Rescuing the Czar

James P. Smythe

Contents

RESCUING THE CZAR

BY

James P. Smythe

FOREWORD
by
W.E. Aughinbaugh, M.D., LL.B., LL.M.

Is the former Czar and his Imperial family still alive? There are millions of people in Europe and America who are asking this question.

European governments have considered the question of sufficient interest to justify the investigation by official bodies of the alleged extinction of this ancient Royal Line. Millions have been expended for that purpose. Commissions have pretended to investigate the subject after *the event. Volumes have been returned of a speculative nature to authenticate a mysterious* disappearance that has never been explained.

April 5; the Universal Service carried a cable from Paris reading: "Czar Nicholas and all members of the Imperial family of Russia are still alive, according to M. Lassies, former member of the Chamber of Deputies, who has just returned from a mission to Russia." This was several weeks after the manuscript of the following account of the Czar's Escape was in my possession.[1] Yet this confirmation of the manuscript has not sufficiently overcome the universally persistent doubt that has grown out of many previous imposing reports.

In certain Royal quarters the anxiety to disseminate the "reports" of their Commissions is too apparent to authorize a judicial mind to accept their speculative guesswork as convincing evidence of a legal corpus delicti *when no identified bodies have ever been produced. This eagerness to convince the world by substituting a mere* disappearance, or the lack of evidence, for positive proof of the Royal assassination raises very naturally the presumption that certain circles are

---

1 February 20, 1920

more interested in misleading than in satisfying the public mind.

To those schooled in the methods and objects of international propaganda during the Great War it is evident that, in a period of revolution, when thrones and dynasties become unpopular within the area of hostility and discontent, the adherents of Royalty may not be unwilling to appease the demand for vengeance by some theatrical display of meeting it with a pretense or an artifice until the passions of the populace have subsided and sober toleration resumes its sway over the sated revolutionary mind.

That such may be the fact will seem convincing from a careful study of the incidents narrated in the following rudimentary story of "Rescuing the Czar." In a technical sense it is not a story. Nevertheless, while partaking of the nature of a simple diary, it reads like a romance of thrilling adventure upon which a skilful novelist may easily erect a story of permanent interest and universal appeal. But it is this very lack of art--this indifference to accomplished technique--that makes "Rescuing the Czar" so interesting and so convincing a rebuttal of the Royal Executioners' Case.

There have been many periods in the progress of society when such an original piece of work as "Rescuing the Czar" would have been welcomed by the historian of serious events. The preservation, discovery and the piecing together of the various scraps of first-hand information by the actual participants in the tragic scenes narrated in these diaries, by the compiler of this book represent a work of so discriminating a judgment that its contribution to the historical wealth of the period involved will assume an increasing, if not a prophetic, value as time goes on, either to explain the mystery or authenticate the evidence revealed. While apparently no connection is evident between the two authors of the First and Second Parts of "Rescuing the Czar," the discriminating reader will be impressed by the independent way each of them, operating unconsciously of the other, sustains the manifest conclusion that both are recording international secrets that never were intended for the public eye.

Imbedded in the national consciousness of many European States the historian finds everywhere the shadowy outlines of "nobility" and "aristocracy" delineated on the surface of traditionary pretense and political desire. It forms the inheritance of distributive power in nations ascending from monarchial institutions to theoretical republics or pseudo-democracies, and it imparts a touch of pathos to the lingering hope of Royalty that humanity may some day welcome its return to reverence and power. It forms the superstructure on which the crumbling column of aristocracy sustains its capital pretensions amid the ruins of privileged exemption from the universal law of change. Consequently the reader will not be surprised nor much alarmed when encountering its subterranean methods depicted in these pages. They will merely fortify the accepted impression among students of events that when Time binds up the wounds of Revolutionary Russia the world will discover an Agrarian Democracy, instead of a Soviet Communism or Romanoff Empire, emerging from the cosmos of organized disorder in that land. This seems to be the trend of thought behind "Rescuing the Czar." Yet it does not conceal a fundamental inclination to sympathize with every rank that suffers in this onward sweep of power. Royalty and Rags, throughout these pages, find many mourners over the sacrifices each has made to reconcile the eternal conflict between poverty and pomp. In the abysmal void between the disappearing star and the aspiring glowworm men tramp upon, there seems to be sufficient latitude for the play of gratitude or grief. A Napoleon exiled by the French or a Ney shot down by Frenchmen is unthinkable today. In like manner, when the revolutionary passions of Russia have subsided, there may be men and women of the humblest estate who will wonder how it happened that their Emperor, whose darkest sin, apparently, was loyalty to Russia, could have been murdered by their countrymen in cold blood.

It will never be believed.

In reflecting on the experiments of their Revolution, finding much to be admired and more to be condemned, they will not accept without resentment an accusation from posterity that they lacked both gratitude and pity when the test of national manhood came. In exculpation of such an imputation they will doubtless reverence the tradition of a House that fell only with the ruins of their native land. Viewing as they may the fragments of their once majestic Empire annexed to alien States in compensation of successful perfidy and neglect, they will lament the lot of Nicholas II while reflecting on their fate. If their democracy shall survive their own self-amputation, the lightness of their governmental burdens will stimulate the flow of mercy through their social institutions and direct their thoughts toward pity for the useless sacrifice.

In simple justice, therefore, "Rescuing the Czar" is offered in extenuation of this doubtful charge against the entire Russian race. For nothing is better calculated to sanctify a martyrdom and make a race abhorred than a belief in its injustice. Nothing is more potent to dissolve a race and scatter its suspected members from the altar of their fathers than the fable of their unrepentant hostility to the cry of Mercy from the sacrificial Ikon. Nothing so quickly exposes their abandoned fields to the tramp of hostile feet and the subjugation of their soil. Ambitious rivalry has no better ally than unexplained suspicion.

If "Rescuing the Czar" does no more than set at rest the fable of the "Romanoff Execution," it will have done its work by characterizing the source and methods and objects of its inspiration. If it raises the presumption of generosity in quarters generally subject to suspicion, it will be equally praiseworthy for expelling the darkness that has always hovered around Imperial thrones. If it does nothing but portray the dignified composure of Russian womanhood in the presence of unspeakable affronts, it will have justified its publication by adding to the diadem of virtue a few more jewels to glorify the crest of motherhood. If it performs no other service than to place upon the pale face of tragic possibility the red-pink blush of romantic probabilities, it will have justified its presence in the society of the learned by the sincerity of its purpose and the candor of its appeal to the conscience of the world.

New York, 1920.

I
FROM SPLENDOR TO GLOOM

The ice was breaking up along the river Neva, in 1917. At the Winter Palace, the ladies were rejoicing over the good news. The Czar in the field was re-organizing his dismembered armies. America was severing diplomatic re-lations with the Central Powers. The Asquith Ministry had dissolved and Lloyd-George was hurling his dynamic personality into organizing Victory for the Allied forces in the field. Kut-el-Amara had fallen to the British--Bagdad had been taken--the Crescent was fleeing before the Cross of Russia--the Grand Duke was driving the Turk from Trebizond. Even Hindenburg was retiring along the West-ern Front--France with unexampled gallantry was holding back the Juggernaut--America was getting mad and rolling up its sleeves.

The women at the palace did not disguise their happiness over the cheerful events that heralded the approach of Victory. The evening star that poured down its steel-blue rays upon the crosses of St. Isaac's presaged to their encouraged fan-cies the early dawn of peace. Yet the chilly wind that whistled round their dull-red household was laden with a frosty air that blew from official regions and "froze the genial current of their souls." The icy glances of ambitious princelings, reflecting back the sinister sullenness of designing ministers, fell like a spectral gloom upon their happy hearts. A hollow roar rolled down the Nevskii Prospekt--a guard burst into the palace and put the women under arrest. The pent-up Revolution at last had burst--anarchy howled around the capital--the isolated Czar was captive, and plot-ting princelings joined hands with puny lawyers to browbeat courageous women and drive the chariot of State!

The miserable fiasco of a delirious Revolution went careering through the giddy maze of treachery and madness until a frenzied wave of rapine and disorder swept all the noblewomen of the Imperial household into a barricaded fortress around which lust and inebriety held unsated and remorseless vigil for the prize. (See Part II: Tumen.)

Among these prisoners of State were five women who realized that the Power which had organized disorder as a feature of its military strategy had also honeycombed the Army, the Navy and the State with its agencies of pillage and so undermined the public conscience that their purity and virtue, more than their jewels and fortune, became an open challenge to the vanity of mob lust.

The younger of these women in their unsullied maidenhood looked longingly and unsuspectingly in the direction of Siberia. They were learning by degrees that the semblance of freedom which offered a pathway to escape was nothing but a strategem employed by pretended friends to entrap them into more cruel and ruthless hands. On every side loomed the evidence of their danger. The villainous stares of foreign interlopers, the ribald jests of guards, the furtive glances of the envious, the scowls of the emancipated underling, the profanity of the domineering agitator who denounced respectability and clamored for possession of the girls,--no moment of their lives was free from ugly threats; no retreat, save the wild jungle or the mountains, offered any liberation from the immodest glare of cruel, licentious eyes. (See Part II: Tobolsk.)

The eldest of the girls was scarcely twenty-two. Like her mother, she was erect and stately and somewhat saddened by the hostile experiences through which the family had just passed. The youngest was a chummy little creature of sixteen years who did not conceal her admiration for her next elder sister, whose courage seemed unfailing through all the trying hours. The next eldest sister, with her little younger brother, was openly planning to outwit the guard and escape to the Siberian wilds. It was doubtless her undisguised activity that ultimately betrayed the Royal prisoners into the unhappy tangle that beset their future lives.

From one camp to another they were carted off like cattle and never for a moment permitted to forget that, if they ever reached a place of safety, they would have to pay the price. Along the frozen pathway of their weary eastern journey there did come, here and there, some slender little byways that offered an escape. Whenever they approached these places and estimated the perils, they found no one to confide in--there were none that they could trust. Treason, like a contagion, lurked in smiles as well as scowls about them, and even their steadfast trust in the Invisible Diplomacy of European Royalty was gradually yielding in their hearts to the dissolving acid of despair. (See Part II: Tobolsk.)

From the conflicting rumors that reached them they fully realized that it was the politician in all countries who ignorantly obstructed their relief. The ferocious and misleading propaganda employed to fanaticize the populace as an element of military strategy seemed to sweep its own authors from their feet and drag the prisoners through many months of torture toward a time and place set for their execution by other politicians in the drunken stupor of their power. (See Part II: Tobolsk.)

Under the agitated surface of this tidal wave of fanaticism that threatened to engulf the Royal prisoners there were a few men in Europe and America, as well as in India and Thibet, who were slowly converging in the direction of the victims with a phrase upon their lips that none but Royalty and themselves were privileged to use. It was that ancient secret code transmitted by tradition to the followers of a sturdy Tyrian king. It was made use of by Lycurgus, as well as by Solomon and Justinian; and it was again employed by the partisans of Louis XVIII to save the House of Bourbon. It is that mystic code which binds Royalty together and is given only to those whom Royalty may trust. That ancient code meant freedom if it reached the prisoners in time! It rested with these silent men to pass the scrutiny of a million eyes to liberate the victims from the fury of the mob.

Such a rescue, as time swept by, became nothing but a slender hope with any of the women. They began to realize that their blood would not very greatly shock the nerves of statesmen who had become accustomed to the daily cataract that poured down upon the soil of Europe. They felt abandoned by the diplomats. Their only friends were busy in the red work of war. One chance alone remained. Soldiers might be deceived by men disguised as comrades. The Secret Service might overlook the hysterical entertainers who fluttered under the mask of charitable workers and skipped across forbidden lines protected by a Cross. This was the only possibility, this the phantom hope that stood trembling on the brink of the prisoners' abysmal fear. Thus the sight of a Red Cross driver or an English uniform in the midst of their disaster became a welcome incident in the lives of these affronted women. The appearance of either seemed to carry to the prisoners a spirit of encouragement and reflect a ray of mercy into the dark corners of their hearts. They indulged the hope that some of those foreign uniforms might conceal trustworthy friends. And they recognized a basis for such a hope in the mystifying movements of one of those uniforms that met their notice day by day. It was near them at the palace when they were thrown upon a maddened world. They saw it following onward as they passed through pathless wilds. They could see it hovering near them on that last historic night. They learned about its maneuvers in the morning as it moved among the silent rooms of the pretty mansard cottage that had witnessed their withdrawal from the vision of historical events,--how it had paused to scan without emotion the small blood stain on the floor--how an agitated censor informed the credulous that the prisoners had been murdered in cold blood! Thus they learned that the world had heard with skepticism that, so far as history and international politicians were affected, their seven lives had been, technically, blotted out! (See Part II: Petrograd--Tumen--Tobolsk.)

Possibly the Prisoners of Tobolsk may have been willing to suffer what is termed a "technical death" in diplomatic circles in order to elude the hungry blood-hounds of the Revolution. They may have welcomed the many opportunities such an event would furnish to read their own obituary in the letters and official documents which treated of their tragic fate. Who knows? They certainly possessed a saving sense of humor or they would never have left behind them at Ekaterinburg so many little reminders of the tragic romance to which calm investigation hereafter will give birth. For instance, there are a couple of diaries that some men must have kept. Of their existence it seems certain that some of the prisoners knew. Why and just how the hitherto profound State secrets narrated in these diaries come now to light is suggested by a simple little letter that raises the inquiry, "Did the Imperial Russian family escape?"

The letter that started this investigation is little different from others one receives from friends traveling in the Orient. By itself it does not clearly identify the family it describes; but, when the scene it pictures is coupled with the events narrated in the purloined diaries which the hands of some invisible diplomats have left behind, the student of the Russian Revolution will marvel at the skill with which some other Royal hands untied the knot of Fate.

II
WHAT MAY BE READ BETWEEN THE LINES

There may be those in official circles who will suggest that a case of mistaken identity is exhibited in the following quotation from the letter. "It is in a sort of arboreal enclosure, with all sorts of flowers and vigorous vegetation that characterizes this region," the letter reads. "Behind the ivy-covered wall that extends around the gardens and shuts out all intruders, I got a glimpse of that man through the heavy iron gate. He was smooth-shaven, slightly drooped, sprinkled with gray and with a scar upon his forehead near the roots of his hair--a little to one side. He was twirling a pruning knife in his left hand and speaking in English to a boy who scampered up to him ahead of four beautiful girls and a very dignified woman moving leisurely over the lawn in the direction of the gate.

"When the women reached the man's side they paused for a moment and asked a few questions in Russian. He seemed to be listening very attentively and answering only in monosyllables.

"Then I noticed the elder of the women unfold a well-known London newspaper and move closer to his side. They began glancing over its pages together and seemed to be deeply moved by an article they, apparently, were reading as they walked slowly toward the gate. Finally, when they were about ten feet from where I stood concealed behind one of the massive palms, the man raised his head from the page and, looking earnestly into the woman's eyes, exclaimed in a skeptical tone: ' Il n'aurait jamais cru le fait si ces messieurs n'avaient pu lui jurer L'avoir vu!... Tout ce que j'ai predit!... Les faux nobles,--les plagiaires!' which means in English, "He couldn't have believed the thing unless these gentlemen had sworn they witnessed it!... All that I predicted!... The sham nobles!... the stealing authors!" The comment set me thinking.

"Who is he? I asked myself. Inside of five minutes I had heard him speak in English, in Russian and in French! I am certain that he is not a Frenchman,--although his accent would have proclaimed him a native of the Avenue des Champs Elysees. He had a Danish countenance, the eyes of English Royalty and the forehead of an early Christian martyr.

"No one I have talked to on the island seems certain of his identity. Some take the view that he is a retired millionaire, judging from the refined simplicity of his family and the strict guard the Government has furnished to protect his undisturbed retirement. Others hint that he may be, possibly, some very high dignitary, judging from the almost Royal homage that some people in the city pay to his person and family.

"The only reliable information I got about him was that he arrived upon the island aboard a man-o'-war accompanied by one of the richest tea merchants in the Empire. He declines all membership in any of the clubs, apparently satisfied to spend the time among his orchids and the lovely white-robed debutantes I saw blooming in that fascinating garden.

"Naturally I was very curious about the identity of this secluded family. But the only information given out about them by the chivalrous tea merchant or the Government officials is simply, 'Oh, the family have friends in India and are living in retirement.'"

One would be very bold to say, after reading the foregoing, that the personages described were the same people who had been driven out of the Winter Palace upon the ebb-tide of their Imperial splendor a few months before. Yet a long and somewhat intimate interest in the underground diplomacy of the world will lead one thus engaged to piece together stray bits of gossip that come from different sources to check up the information that some others may possess. In this way will the letter of an American who was held incommunicado at Geneva by the Swiss Government in the latter part of 1919, be found exceedingly persuasive in the process of reconstructing the tragic comedy which struts around the vacant Russian throne. The American was en route to Turkestan under proper credentials from the United States; yet there were certain powerful combinations sufficiently interested in his mission to cause his imprisonment for a time sufficiently lengthy to enable their emissaries to precede him beyond the Caspian, where other secret combinations were incubating that American foreign traders would have given much to understand.

It was during this period of restraint that the American, whose name we will call Fox, wrote to a friend in the United States: "You have often heard me speak of my brother who was in Turkestan when the Russian Revolution burst upon the world. He is now resting in Tasmania after going through one of the most remarkable experiences ever given to an ordinary tea merchant *intrusted with some secrets of* the greatest land monopoly in the world. You may call it a fairy tale; and if you did not know me as a business man of ordinary sense, I should hesitate to intimate that Nicholas R---- and all the family are quite well, I thank you, not a million miles distant from my brother."

Fox had learned from his experience at Geneva that governments are sometimes cajoled by diplomatic pressure to do undreamed-of things. The dispatch of an expeditionary force to Siberia by the United States without a declaration of war against the Revolutionists struck him as an instance of this kind, and he knew his correspondent to be sufficiently versed in the underground politics of Europe to look for a connection between some member of that expedition and the subject mentioned in the two foregoing letters. This connection was innocently revealed by a newspaper report from a Western city concerning a wounded soldier who had recently returned to an American Army hospital. The particular name being given, it was easy enough for Fox's correspondent to meet the soldier on some errand of mercy and to obtain the revelations that are hereinafter made.

The soldier was a young commissioned officer who was having an artificial jaw supplied to replace the one shot off in a Bolshevik encounter. He had greatly recovered when the call was made and an opening naturally presented for the soldier to recount the part he played in the adventure of his country in the Revolutionary drama of that hour.

"I'm as certain as I'm living," the wounded soldier said, "that a Bolshevik is as 'nutty' as a rabbit. The fellow I had by the neck before my lights went out was putting up a holler, in German, and claiming to be a personal friend of some personal friend of the missing Czar. Before he finally passed in his chips he gave me a bundle of paper diaries he had stolen down in China, and he asked me to return them to their rightful owner so that he might die without a sin upon his conscience. Honestly, that chap was dead in earnest in this matter of his conscience. I took the stuff, of course; but I never thought about them until the other day. Since then they seem to haunt me. I wonder if you'd mind looking them over if the nurse'd get them out?"

"With pleasure," was the reply.

The nurse brought in an old leather bag, from which the Captain extracted two begrimed and blood-smeared rolls written in a very small but strong and vigorous hand.

While looking over the documents in a casual way a loose leaf fell to the floor. Upon picking it up, there was found to be written on one side in bold underscored letters:

> "Make no belief in the evidence that was manufactured to
> satisfy some bloodthirsty men in Russia. What I have seen with
> my own eyes I know is true. For the sake of Russia I stoled
> these papers from the man come from the West who was with them
> all the way from 'Yekaterinburg to Chunking. What he write is
> true.
>
> "DONETSKY"

"That's his name," the Captain said, "and if you don't find that he was as crazy as a bedbug I'll say I'm General Graves."

"This diary seems to be written in very good English."

"Yes," said the Captain, "all those fellows keep one. They're like the Germans--give 'em a pencil and a piece of paper and they'll scribble all day."

"Did he say who wrote this?"

"No; he cashed in, as I told you; but you'll see the name of Fox here and there through the diary that's written in the small hand."

"Fox--who was 'Fox'?"

"Search me! Some Johnny, I suppose."

"May I take these with me?"

"Sure thing! I'll make you a present of 'em. All I ask is, if you find out whether that fellow 'Fox' grabs the peacherino from the Metropole or the one called 'Maria' you'll send me an invitation."

The bargain was struck. Then the question was asked: "Any idea who wrote this diary--the one written in a quick running hand?'

"Sounds like some fellow with a grouch against Kerensky and Lvov. I know enough Russian to make out that much--"

"Evidently one of the Revolutionary officials?"

"Seems so," the Captain said. "You'll notice what he has to say about the mixup with the Russian Royal family at Tobolsk and Tumen. There's a lot of our fellows who don't take any stock in that assassination business at 'Katerinburg.'"

"I began to read: 'I had walked from Euston Station to Madame Tussaud's, when the messenger jumped from his motorcycle and rushed up to me--' Your diarist starts out in London, I see."

"Yes, he is some globe trotter--"

""Go to Birdcage and walk slowly back to Queen Victoria Memorial. As you pass Buckingham, observe the heavily veiled lady wearing white lace wristlets who will follow on behind. Let her overtake you. If she utters the correct phrase, go with her at once to Admiralty Arch and follow the Life Guard to the War Office. Meet number ... there; receive a small orange-colored packet, wear the shirt he gives you, and cross the Channel at once'"--I see! From Buckingham Palace to the War Office; sounds interesting."

"It is; that fellow is all there!" complimented the Captain.

"'The meeting at the Huis ten-Bosch *points to Wilhelmstrasse. Nothing can be done here. They suspect Downing Street.'--Ah, at The Hague, and at the* ten-Bosch too, where the Czar and Andrew Carnegie held their first Peace Conference in 1899; this looks significant!"

"Keep going," said the Captain; "that fellow's got 'The Man in the Iron Mask' brushed off the map."

"Here is something singular about Berlin. Your man walks through the lines like a wraith--"

"Not always. As you get into his stuff you'll hear things sizzle."

And thus the Imperial dead return to life through the pages of these stolen diaries.

While the temptation is great to revise the manuscript, so as to make it read more smoothly, it has been decided not to alter a line or letter. Truth will be better served by publishing what is prudent, under the complicated political circumstances of our times, word *for* word as it was written by its daring author.

III
WHAT HAPPENED AT BERLIN

For certain persuasive reasons it is deemed prudent to omit that part of the diary which details the writer's experiences in England, Belgium and Holland. Those who recognize the incidents hereafter given will appreciate this act of censorship. The discerning reader will gain all the information necessary by following the "Invisible Diplomat" and author from Berlin to the end of the diary.

The first entry reads:

"Today I called on Count R---- at Thiergartenstrasse 23 and handed him the yellow packet. Then I went with him to the race track at Hoppegarten.... On the way out R. inquired about the incident at Buckingham and asked me if I were willing to continue the adventure.... I assured him that nothing would please me better, providing the lady *was good-looking.... He said that there were more than ONE lady as well as a couple of men involved in the affair.... I replied that if there were enough to go around and the men didn't become too meddlesome, their presence wouldn't spoil the 'adventure.'... He assured me that the men were 'fine fellows,' the ladies the loveliest on earth, but the 'adventure' was one that might mean decapitation for me if I failed in the undertaking.... I told him that just suited me.... 'I expect to meet Colonel Z---- S---- von T---- at the track. If he takes a liking to you he'll invite you to Koenigergratzerstrasse for a quiet little talk,' Count R---- replied after I had climbed up on the box with him.... We had just reached the old saddle paddock when a man saluted us in a very* knowing manner.... It was Colonel Z---- S----, who put some pointed questions to me about my recent travels and my knowledge of Oriental languages.... Before returning to the hotel tonight the Colonel asked me to call on him tomorrow.... I feel that his request amounts to a positive command.... I shall call early in the morning...."

4. On the same page the following entry was made:

"There were guards everywhere when I called at K-70. Even the doorkeeper was a non-com, who took my name, entered it in a book with the precise time I called, took down his telephone, merely mentioned my name, hung up the receiver, called an orderly who conducted me through a corridor and three anterooms full of civilian clerks and finally landed me in the private office of Colonel Z---- S----. He wore the undress uniform of the Imperial Army, greeted me pleasantly, offered me a cigar and tactfully asked: 'Have you positively made up your mind to continue in this service?'

"I wanted to know a little more fully what was required of me before answering; but he did not say. He insisted, rather, on my answering his question FIRST.... To be perfectly frank I was not anxious to commit myself unreservedly without knowing ALL he expected of me, but it sounded cowardly ... so with a mental reservation *I finally said: 'You don't look like a man who would ask another to commit suicide. Go ahead! I've decided to take a chance.'... Colonel Z---- S---- looked me straight in the eye and said: 'We expect you to use the same tactics that are used against you. We can't be squeamish.... The interests at stake are too* sacred *to allow personal considerations to affect your conduct.... You will be required to undertake a journey in the capacity of a guide.... How you make it will be left entirely to yourself* ... but we expect results.... Every resource will be placed at your disposal, but if YOU get into trouble *you'll have to get yourself out without calling on us for help.... We* must not *be known in the matter. And understand this--the assignment is dangerous from start to finish; no official help can be given you under ANY circumstances.'... To get a line on things I asked, casually, what my compensation would be.... He replied: 'You will be allowed a regular retainer fee, an allowance for daily expenses and a* bonus *sufficiently attractive to make the undertaking worth while, as* you *should know.' I thought a little while before asking, 'When do I start?'... 'There's another thing,' he said. 'I suppose you know we* retain one-third of your fee for the benefit of your family in the event of any trouble.'... I merely nodded and said, 'All right.'"

In a moment a clerk brought in a check for 400, which Colonel Z---- S---- gave me, saying: 'This is your first month's allowance for expenses; your retainer will be paid quarterly.'... 'How do you KNOW I won't swindle you?' I asked, being a perfect stranger *to him. 'I am taking my ORDERS from above,' he answered....* 'Who?' I asked. 'Young man!' he thundered, 'learn this QUICK--don't ask questions; keep your ears and eyes open and your mouth SHUT.... Be here at 10 tomorrow.'

5. The next entry of interest read as follows:

"I met Colonel Z---- S---- at 10 today. My head was not clear. Guess I had too much at Kempinsky's last night.... A saturnalia of spending on the theory that the Allies will pay.... Even the ride in the Grunewald this morning didn't clear the cobwebs away. I was constantly thinking of that girl at the Metropole with her long eyelashes and dimpling smile; resembles the veiled lady at Buckingham,--and I was trying to make out why she managed to occupy a seat at the next table to mine at the Admiral's Palace an hour or two later. She seems to know some of the performers who mingled in the audience, especially the energetic dark-eyed Circe with the Greek nose, and said to be some sort of a Baroness, who so often approached my table. I wonder what the connection is between these two.... There is certainly *some sympathetic tie between those girls! This I know, for when I had breakfast at the Cafe Bauer, U.d.L., they were BOTH there, slightly disguised, and occupying* the same table!... Who is Syvorotka? Her lover?... I wonder what the game is.... Come to think about it, the titled performer of the Metropole looks like a twin sister of Marie Amelia, Countess of [Cszecheny] Chechany, a perfect composite of Juno and Venus and Hebe all rolled into one.... These enigmatical personages crowded everything else out of my mind as I walked into Colonel Z---- S----'s office....

"... Without any preliminaries he said, 'Come with me!'... We entered a cab and a few minutes later I entered the Wilhelmstrasse and was in the presence of that tall, iron-gray, wiry gentleman with eyes like a searchlight and the manners of a Chesterfield. 'Thank you, Colonel,' he said. The Colonel sprang to attention, bowed, saluted and backed away. We were ALONE!... 'In ten minutes,' he said, 'you will be conducted to another room. When you arrive advance to the middle, make a right wheel and stand at attention facing the portiere. Maintain perfect silence, answer all question,--make NO inquiries--understand?'... I was taken downstairs, along a wide corridor to a solid-oak door guarded by two sentries and an attendant in the Royal livery. The door was opened by an officer of the Erste Garde; I entered a large room, advanced to the center and faced the divided portieres of an adjoining chamber! There sat the man whose nod shook the earth!... Behind a heavy, old-fashioned desk, in a dim light, apparently absorbed in writing, sat a deeply tanned, lean-faced, blue-gray-eyed counterpart of Frederick the Great,--the very embodiment of Majesty!... Eyes that blazed in their defiant depths with a steady and consuming fire--the kind of eyes that seem to defy the world.... I stood there fully five minutes before I heard the sharp, high-pitched voice pierce through the portiere saying: 'Adell, I will see the C----'... I was conducted to within six feet of the man at the desk and in the same shrill voice asked how familiar I was with Russia, with Turkestan, India, and the Far East.... My answers seemed to convince my questioner.... Handing me a note he said: 'No one besides ourselves is to know that you are to undertake the mission outlined in that note.' Then he sat forward abruptly, his elbows resting on the desk, his head between his hands, his eyes fixed on space.... I began to study the note.... I was dumfounded!... I had thought all along that this man was the mortal enemy of the persons this note commanded me to rescue from danger.... I could not understand HOW there could be the slightest co-operation between this man and the other great ones of the earth that note commanded me to call upon for assistance in case I should need it. It was utterly incomprehensible! Yet THERE were the directions in plain black and white.... And I could not ask a solitary question!... In the same shrill voice the man asked: 'Have you memorized it?' I had! It was burned into my very soul. I could not forget a syllable of it!... Without another word he took the note, struck a match and watched it curl into shapeless ashes.... Then making a quick gesture he plunged into the documents before him.... I backed away until the door closed and shut out the sight of the lonely figure enveloped in a green light, his face illuminated against the shadowy background of an underground chamber of the Foreign Office.... On the way to Friedrichstrasse depot I met that girl of the Metropole again!"

IV
WHEN ROYALTY GETS DOUBLE-CROSSED

6. The next entry was:

"On the Orient Express, or what was the O.E. before the 'Grosse General Stab' took over the whole job of mixing up these schedules.... Well, well, well, the veiled lady of the Metropole and Buckingham is in trouble in the next compartment ... at least so she says!... She just came into my compartment and said she had been insulted by the man who is sharing it with her.... Confound him!... BUT ... Now I've heard of such 'plants' before.... While I'd like to go in there and kick the brute through the partitions I believe discretion is the better part of valor.... Let her call the guard if the case needs attention.... The guard is a reservist and I believe she knows *it.... Furthermore, I must be at Donaustrasse 24, Budapest, tomorrow, and meet Colonel Shuvalov at the Hotel de Paris, Belgrade, the day after.... I wonder if that petit Paris looks the same as when I met my old friend Count Arthur Zu Weringrode and Kazimir Galitzyn coquetting with Cecilia Coursan, Mlle. Balniaux and the Petite Valon at the card tables after our sparkling dinners a few years ago.... And where is that fire-eating Prince now?... He was a great friend of Grey and Churchill at Monte Carlo.... and notwithstanding that meeting in the Taunus they MUST BE friends YET.... The Monte Carlo combination HOLDS good today.... The Taunus meeting so far as Haldane and Winston Spencer were concerned was a* frame-up to catch Waechter and 'His Whiskers' (both the Admiral and the General).... That's where the Wilhelmstrasse FELL DOWN!... and yet I am on a mission of mercy, in behalf of one of the principal double-crossers, today!... Must see Kovalsky at Donau 24 sure.... Mademoiselle must take care of herself today...."

The next entry read:

"This is a great combination--Roumania is sidestepping Wilhelmstrasse.... Greece *is tying up with Servia, Bulgaria is likely to form a wedge between a complete coalition of these mutually hating and suspicious grafters.... Montenegro is the only honest combination in the whole bunch.... In another hour I will see Koval-sky and* astonish him with the news I bring."

7. Then the following entry: "K---- is absolutely opposed *to taking any part in this business.... Will not raise a hand without the sanction of CHARLES.... Looks as though I'll have to bring pressure on these despairing creatures.... They wanted the Balkans,--that was the deal in the Black Forest,--and because some one doesn't hand it to them on a silver platter they complain of der Grosse General Stab's neglect!... At two I get my answer.... If O.K. I'll be in Odessa in 48 hours unless that veiled minx of the Metropole sticks a knife under my fifth rib.... Her conduct is becoming* mighty suspicious!... Watch me give her a run for her money!"

8. Then there was this entry: "Charles refuses to see me but tells K---- not *to put any obstacles in my way.... this is a pretty mess!... How in the devil am I to slip through the lines with those devilish English and French officers scattered around everywhere?... If Roumania had only listened to reason!... I think that Mackinzen will be able to help me out,--I might as well ask Envir Pasha as these dervishes of Sofia to lend a hand in this affair!... Yet I* must, simply MUST be in Odessa in time to meet Vladimir K before the order of execution!... Either that--or jump into the Danube!"

9. The following entry is significant: "I have been deaf, dumb and blind for the last 24 hours! The veiled lady was responsible.... She had me kidnapped and carried out into these infernal hills, wherever they are.... Never saw them before.... Looks as if a cyclone hit them.... One can pick up enough shells and scrap iron to stock a foundry.... The trees are all shot off--nothing but stumps and slivered trees and broken wheels and boxes littered around.... Looks like SOME FIGHT had taken place in this strong-smelling hopyard among these hummocks.... Apparently the hogs have been rooting up the ground all around here.... There isn't a sign of a living thing in sight ... and not a drop of water to be had!... WHO was that woman?... The

Baroness, who?... Must find out more about Syvorotka."

10. "... Been tramping all day in the direction of the rising sun.... Mud, mud, mud everywhere.... It may have been a good thing that I wrote my brother Fox at Mendocino about this trip before I set out.... If I am lost and this comes into a white man's hands who understands America he will know what to do with it.... Hunger and thirst are delirious bed-fellows.... Seems like a hundred years since I heard that Metropole woman's voice when they were choking me in the carriage.... She was saying, 'Search him, search him; I know he ran away with it; it belonged to the Princess!' Then that deep heavy voice: 'What did it look like?' Every word he uttered seemed to add pneumatic pressure to his grip on my neck.... 'It was almost a light purple, the size of a hickory nut, shaped like a pyramid and gives out the re-flection of a cluster of stars,' she cried like a wench.... 'Worth a great deal of money,' the deep voice grunted as his hand pressed harder against my windpipe.... 'Price-less!' she shrieked. 'It couldn't be duplicated for 100,000 rubles; the most gorgeous sapphire in the world!'... 'Are you sure this man has it?'... 'Certainly!' she insisted; 'didn't I see that little wasp Kerensky give it to his cousin, and didn't I see that cous-in give it to this man in America?'... 'Who is this man?' he asked, tightening his grip until my tongue hung out.... 'They call him Fox on the west coast of America; but THAT is NOT his name,' was the last I remember until I found myself lying on the roadside among the hills back yonder.... I certainly DO resemble my brother slight-ly and am hoping that if he has a sapphire the size mentioned by that hissing vixen he will keep it for the honor and glory of the family of Foxes.... And to think that a few days ago I was falling in love with her at the Metropole!... If man is a meditating atom, WOMAN must be a premeditating subterfuge!... I see smoke rising over the hills away to the east.... Yes, it's the smoke of guns.... I can hear the hoarse roar of heavy artillery to the right and the spitting hollow barking and coughing of lighter pieces on the left and I feel the ground quiver as I write these lines."

11. The next entry read:

"What a somersault has taken place in the general slippery coalitions of these capricious provinces! Every Potsdammer, a little while ago, was counting on Rou-mania!... The breaking up of the confederation of the Balkan States under Russian influence was what the Central Powers required; while the Allies desired a broken Turkey and a strong Balkan federation under Russian sway able to throw a million men into the field against Turkey's northwestern frontier so as to keep Austria in check and allow an easy glide of forces toward the Dardanelles.... Then Roumania was with the Wilhelmstrasse, and Bulgaria was an ally of the Quay d'Orsay and the Neva, but now the Osmanlian and the Bulgar and his cousin Fritz are in the same bed snoring at the Romans who look greedily toward Transylvania!... From what I can see I'm sure these Bulgars will be first to give up the ghost, although when I talk to Kovalsky and hear the whine of these Wienfloss Kwabins I feel sure that they will be first to snap for peace!... I am writing this in a elaborately furnished dugout that has been abandoned by some German officers--I KNOW this because I found several tubes of Erbswurst tucked in one of the berths. With a little water I managed to make a good meal which saved my life,--blessed be the Goths or whoever it was who invented those compressed sausages!"

12. The next entry: "I'm becoming worried about the size of this diary ... getting so bulky as to almost prevent concealment in case of capture.... Yet I know a way to prevent detection ... so simple!... Usually the most elaborate effort at concealment leads to detection while the most obvious and simple will be entirely overlooked.... I'll try it and if it goes through I'll patent it!... SOMEONE IS COMING--sounds like a dozen auto-trucks!... No, it's an aeroplane *skirmishing mighty close to my headquarters.... They've* landed and are coming this way!... I'll be READY for them...."

V

WHEN TITLED WOMEN STOOP TO CONQUER

13. The next entry:

"My ammunition was no good!... But I am at a loss to understand what they are trying to do with ME.... Certainly I don't look like a very important personage in my present state.... Yet my captors are not treating me very badly ... aside from being locked up in this deserted villa with its broken chairs and vacant picture frames and general air of hasty abandonment there's nothing to disturb the tranquillity of my reflections except the recurring tramp of the muffled sentry below my broken window ... this building has a sort of Byzantine cut in its architectural design.... On the other side of the valley there's a minaret or two visible through the smoky haze.... Off to the left I can make out quite distinctly the outlines of a Greek Cross.... The road leading toward that Cross looks like the work of a Muscovite engineer,-- which speaks well for it.... It's built of the same material as the one over the mountains from Tiflis to Vladicaucaz and Kislovodsk.... I MUST BE ON RUSSIAN SOIL!... But what is mystifying *to me is,* how did that veiled girl *of the Metropole manage to know the SENTRY who is guarding my person so methodically down below?... She has been here twice, now, and talks to him very confidentially.... QUATSCH! if she thinks to find* any jewelry clinging to my person she'll have to fry me to get it out."

14. Then this entry:

"The veiled Metropole Nemesis was to see the sentry today.... She seemed to be quite happy about something and looked up in the direction of my window a number of times.... She was eating some of those champagne-colored rose leaves that are crystallized by the firm of Demitrof at Moscow and sold as confections to the ladies of the Court!... What does it mean?... Furthermore, if that sentry is not the same man who acted as valet to Prince Galitzyn at Monte Carlo when Delcasse, Grey and Galitzyn (otherwise "Count Techlow") were gliding about the Grand Hotel de Londres!

"The mystery is solved....

"That Metropole woman was the companion to Countess C---- at the Nouvel Hotel Louvre the day I met her at Monte Carlo!... and this man was the same *fellow she was supping her cafe Turc and smoking her Medijeh cigarettes with out on the Terrace Gardens of the Hotel de Londres the night I was waiting for an American millionaire to break away from the Hungarian noblewoman at the table decorated with La France roses and the same kind of roses pinned to her corsage.... The American, if he ever sees this in print, will remember the lady with the wonderful jewels flashing from her wrists and neck and whom the man with the Boulanger moustache at the adjoining table was trying hard to flirt with ... the same dark-eyed Juno that same American met in the Salle des Etrangers at the Casino, the following day about noon.... Well, that is the connection!... But I did not observe that that wonderful lady wore any large SAPPHIRE that night ... nor when she changed her quarters from the* Nouvel *to the* London *did she need any such jewelry to have all the spendthrifts of Europe at her feet.... If she was a 'Princess' then I was completely fooled.... I never saw a real Princess, except* Eulalia, who knew how to be democratic enough to select an American for a quiet exchange of ideas ... the rest, no matter how desperately they may want to be free from Court restraint and bodyguards, remind me of the poor little caged girls at the Convent of the Sacred Heart at Seville!... Well, so my captors have some connection with the Countess C----([Cszecheny] Chechany)--with the Tolna Festetics of Hungary.... And this is strange, for I had surmised that SHE, at least, would be friendly *to MY mission, if she knows anything at all about its origin....* She *should* aid me to reach Odessa instead of having me sandbagged and cooped up here in this Soviet cage.... I'm certain this Metropole lady is a TRAITOR to the Countess now, and will have me murdered if I don't produce that sapphire of the princess."

15. This entry may serve to identify the author of the diary:

"I am certain that the former occupant of this villa was some Russian of taste and means. Today, while leaning against a wall that was paneled after the fashion of the walls in the Hermitage, one of the panels gave way and I found myself toppling backward into a very large room resembling a gallery. There were a number of wall hangings of silk from which the pictures had been removed. The candelabra was of malachite. There were clumps of violet jasper, porphyry, lapis-lazuli, aventurine and syenite scattered around as though the place had been divested of its furnishings in a hurry. I have seen the same things in the HERMITAGE when for architectural elegance, richness of ornamentation and lavishness of decoration it was unequaled by any art museum in the world.... While poking around among the piles of tables and vases that were moved over to one corner I came across a box of paintings that must have been STOLEN from St. Petersburg.[2] ... Here is the Madonna del Latte *of Corregio, or a mighty good imitation, that everyone remembers, from the Hermitage. Here is Rembrandt's* 'Girl with the Broom,' the Portrait of Sobieski, and the 'Farmyard' of Paul Potter. Here is the 'Expulsion of Hagar' by Rubens in which Sarah wears a white handkerchief and yellow veil around her head, with one of her hands resting on her hip and the other encased in a blue sleeve raised in a threatening gesture toward Hagar, and here is 'Celestine and her Daughter in Prison,' that one NEVER forgets because of the controversy between the partisans of Murillo and Velasquez over which of these two painters did the work. And here is Lossenke's 'Sunrise on the Black Sea,' Ugrimov's 'Capture of Kazan' and 'Election of Michael Romanov,' in which the artist reaches the heights of Oriental splendor in color, composition and design.... There is a FORTUNE going to the devil in this room!... This house is L-shaped. The garden in the rear faces a pretentious two-story dwelling surrounded by a wall, like a Governor General's mansion in its yellow-pinkish coat. Tall poplar trees wave in front and the classic columns running up to the entablature give the place an official sort of front. There is a drug store on the corner across the way doing business under the name of Torkiani. To the right, at the end of the street, is a girls' college; to the left, about 800 feet away, in the center of the street, is the Alexander Nevsky Church, if I'm not very much mistaken. This city must have been a wonder before the war...." Then this entry: "Something is about to happen!... My sentry seems very excited over the desertion 'on Ekaterine Street' and

2   Still the German nomenclature.

swears quite often at the failure of some one to appear 'along the Levashov.'"

16. This entry may explain the difficulty:

"There is an Army Corps approaching from the southwest.... The air is surcharged with electricity and puts one's nerves on edge.... There is an ominous roar overhead that grows more nerve-racking every second.... Zip, zip, zip, bl-r-r-r-oo-ow!... A flock of Foelkers heading east like wild ducks toward a few faint specks zigzagging in the firmament away to the northeast.... Now there are a number of specks from the south speedily joining these and ALL seem to be flitting higher and higher out of sight.... Now the Foelkers are circling rapidly upward.... The tramp and rattle of an Army can be heard coming up the road behind my villa.... Ah! here comes a daring plane like a streak of lightning over the Alex Nevsky Church directly toward this prison!... I'm between the Devil and the Deep Sea!... Whoever gets me, that flyer or those noisy and unseen dogs of war back yonder, means nothing but plain HELL to ME!..."

17. The next entry is interesting:

"Well, I'm not DEAD yet!... A trip through the clouds is NOT the most delightful of experiences for one in summer togs.... Especially when one is gagged and blindfolded and roped down like a rebellious steer.... So here I am cooped up again in a log cabin in the center of an undulating plain where there might have been unending wheat fields once upon a time.... Not a solitary animal is in sight.... The road out yonder looks much the worse for wear. It seems ground into a pumice stone by the hoofs of horses and the swift movement of heavy wheels. Every gust of wind sends a cloud of fine dust pyramiding its way across the fields and through the crevices of this suffocating den furnished with a few wooden chairs, a hand-carved bedstead, a small picture of the 'Virgin of the Partridges' and a brass crucifix above the bed.... I greatly SUSPECT my present whereabouts.... I am as much mystified as ever why that veiled Metropole Circe continues to dog my FLIGHTS.... It was she who was the daring flyer and she beat the whole army getting to my retreat in that neglected villa and spiriting me away...."

VI
THE LADY AND THE FIRING SQUAD

18. This looks exciting:

"I must jot down this experience: When I was taken from the log cabin I was blindfolded and again strapped into a flying machine. There were half a dozen soldiers present; and ONE was certainly an ENGLISHMAN,--I had heard his voice before. I NEVER forget a voice. If his eyes ever meet these lines he will remember me, I know. I can describe him from memory. He was medium height, wore a drooping moustache slightly sprinkled with gray and used two pairs of tortoise-shell glasses. When I met him at The Pines in the Isle of Wight we had both been through the Battle of the Somme and were recuperating from our siege amid the shell holes and the mud. I CLAIMED to be an American, and he, as a descendant of the victor of Trafalgar, scolded me roundly and vicariously *for not forcing the United States into the war on the side of Britain,--he'll remember* that.... Perhaps it was because he DID recognize me that he insisted on my being blindfolded and handled roughly when I was led away.... The rest of the squad spoke FRENCH very poorly.... They asked me a number of questions, to which I shook my head; and, candidly, I could do so without doing violence to my knowledge of idiomatic French!... I heard them say to one another, 'When we get him to the stockade we'll see what he is made of.' 'Yes; a firing squad'll be the best thing for ALL of them.' 'Certainly! we'll follow Machiavelli's recommendation in The Prince,--EXTERMINATE the whole race!' That's the idea! There should be no Louis XVIII bobbing up a generation from now to overthrow the democracy.'... To be honest with my conscience I felt creepy.... I really wanted to tell them that they had got the WRONG FELLOW, but when I tried to speak my tongue felt so dry and thick that I could not utter an audible word.... so I remained involuntarily silent.... Well, on this flight I was more comfortable than on the last; but I thought it would never end and I felt horribly SEASICK.... Finally I was landed and hustled into a court made from the ends of small logs pegged into the ground like an improvised palisade,--it was in a little village....

"... There were hundreds of tatterdemalians of all nations in various uniforms and smoking vile cigarettes, lounging carelessly around.... In a little while a dozen prisoners issued from a small guardhouse in one corner of the enclosure and were conducted at the point of the bayonet to the spot where I stood.... The officer of this firing squad looked viciously at me and ordered me to 'fall in.'... We were then marched to the log wall about fifty paces to the left of the guardhouse and commanded to 'about face.'... When we did so we saw a firing squad of eighteen men in command of a Sergeant who gave the order 'Prepare to fire!'... At this point the officer stepped forward and, addressing me personally, said: 'Do you know of any reason why you should not be shot for participating in the abduction of the Imperial family?'... This was a puzzler.... I was innocent enough of such an accusation, BUT the officer before me looked about as much like a Royalist as I in my present disheveled condition looked like a member of the French Cabinet.... If I denied my guilt I felt certain of a bullet in my heart from such an ugly, unkempt mob.... Glancing at my apparel I looked fit to be one of their number, so I said courageously: 'I am PROUD to say that I am the ringleader who engineered the whole business!...'"

If it gives you any satisfaction to see me die, don't waste your breath asking me any further questions,--go ahead and fire!'... 'Very well,' he snapped and made me about-face to the firing squad ... For a few seconds he held a silent conversation with the Sergeant.... That functionary approached with a handkerchief. 'Will you be blindfolded?' he asked. 'Thank you, I prefer to see what's going on,' I answered.... The other prisoners followed my example.... We were ordered to step back against the wall.... The squad raised their rifles at the command of 'aim.'... I now know that I felt positively nauseated at the moment, but I actually SMILED.... 'Fire!'... There was a rattle of musketry and every prisoner beside me fell forward dead.... I STOOD THERE ALONE, uninjured and alive ... coming toward me down the path was the daring female acrobatic aviator with her friend, the performer of the Metropole, robed in a shimmering sport outing costume, and smiling very sweetly to the Officer of the Guard....

"... I am certain now that this veiled lady from Buckingham is in league with this gang of Bolsheviki,--and I am also certain that I owe my life to the boast I made of being a murderer myself!..."

19. The following entry reads:

"A man who has escaped death is not to be trusted on a point of discretion,--he doesn't know how to select his friends. He is like a spirit emerging from nowhere in the eternal void and grabs at the first apparition that promises companionship in his embarrassing and momentary isolation.... Well, I was so glad to see that Buckingham Clorinda that I was willing to take her into my confidence at once.... She seemed so sympathetic!... 'I commend your bravery,' she said prettily, offering me her hand.... It was small and beautifully moulded, yet firm and steady, and sent an electric thrill through me like a flash.... Her eyes would disarm the most suspicious diplomatic free-lance in the world.... Struck with admiration, hypnotized by her voice, I could only blurt, 'I thank you.'

"...'We are looking for a man of approved courage,' she continued earnestly; 'we are more than satisfied that YOU are the man.'... Again I muttered my thanks.... 'How long have you been a member?' she then asked carelessly.... THIS was not so easily answered.... I thought quickly.... 'Long enough to KNOW my lesson!' I answered oracularly.... 'You still remember your instructions?'... 'What instructions?' She answered my question by asking, 'Were they not BURNED?'... 'Who is this encyclopaedic lady?' I asked myself. 'What manner of TRAP is she setting for me now?'... 'Why did you SANDBAG me?' was MY answer.... 'You are NOT to ask questions,' she returned. 'Are you not satisfied with results?'...

"... 'I am still alive.'... 'Well,' she smiled, 'a live Bolshevik, of OUR kind, is much better than a dead diplomat!'... I was taken into an improvised kitchen and indulged in a splendid meal.... I took no wine....

"... My meal being finished she *offered me an excellent cigarette.... Glancing up through a ring of smoke my eyes fell upon a rough black-and-white sketch of a tall, smooth-faced, keen-eyed man with rather large ears, firm and thin-cut lips, high forehead and steadfast gaze, dressed in the uniform of a General Officer, with a single decoration on his left breast....* she *observed me closely as I gazed.... I KNEW this man and was about to exclaim:* 'The savior of this country!'... but something restrained my enthusiasm.... 'You recognize him, I see,' she insinuated.... 'WHO is he?' I dodged.... She merely smiled.... She evidently realizes the wonderful power of that disarming smile and the fascination of good teeth in a shapely head.... 'You'll do!' she said with apparent reservation as she tapped a tiny bell....

"... A short, thickset man appeared--he is not positively ugly, but he has a way of staring at one that is rather ill-bred.... There is a gold band around his left wrist and a scar upon his right cheek.... I am sure he is the SAME man I met at one of Sadakichi-Hartmann's readings from Ibsen's Ghosts.... He may recall the time.... It was in an abandoned palace on Russian Hill, somewhere in America; the lady at his left was discussing the difficulties of getting her motor car into Ragiz; the younger one on his right was known as Alma and gave her address as East 61st Street, New York.... and ALL THREE were quite convinced that the Central Powers will defeat the Allies.... He is an international character and will remember this incident as well as the following: '... This gentleman will join your party for Ekaterinburg tonight, YOU understand. If there are any mistakes I shall not answer for results!' There were NO introductions.... The man bowed and began to back away.... 'YOU may accompany him,' she said, rising and flitting from the room.... I believe I understand what this party *means!... There is to be a SHOOTING party at Ekaterinburg under the auspices of the Bolshevists in a day or two and I may be ONE of the* 'mistakes' for which that mystifying lady disclaims responsibility.... My companion certainly looks like a bandit, and manifests the strength of a wild bull.... He seems much interested in that patch on my shirt sleeve...."

VII
THE ROYAL BOLSHEVIK AND THE NURSE

20. "My Charybdis conducted me to the barracks where a lot of undisciplined philosophers were discussing the parceling out of land.... The ringleader was a round-headed, long-nosed and bulky individual with a shaggy beard and dirty uniform.... I knew him in an instant, but he did not recognize me ... he was one of Von der Goltz' men who aided in the defense at Gallipoli.... The night before the Allied fleet withdrew he was lying beside a short, thickset and dark-haired Associated Press reporter with a German name and tortoise-shell eyeglass and was telling that same reporter that unless REINFORCEMENTS arrived AT ONCE the defenses would collapse!... The next day he was at Headquarters informing the General in command that BUT FOR HIM the Turkish forces would have surrendered!... He is NOW wearing a number of decorations for his military skill and bravery.... Such are the fortunes of war!... This is the man who one minute preaches communism and another minute gravely asserts that it will be a good thing for the Kaiser to get killed in the war so as to guarantee the SUCCESSION of the Empire.... Perhaps he is doing this for my benefit.... Anyway he occupies the center of the stage at present and GOVERNS this greedy and unruly mob by kicking discipline into a cocked hat and allowing every unshaved Bolshevik his own unrestricted way!... Under other circumstances I should dearly like to meet this boasting Furioso *in a ten-foot ring when a little exercise is needed to keep myself in trim.... But NOW I am accepted as a BOLSHEVIK,--one of the elect, privileged to select my lady and rob and pillage when I please!...* This suits me very well *... but on mature* reflection *it seems to me that a FEW in this literally UNGODLY gang are playing a very cunning part.... If that BE so I am* not *so sure how far my own assumed conversion to*

the doctrine of rapine will protect my skin.... So far, however, I have adopted the policy of vindictiveness, and, when asked a question, I merely growl and swear like a trooper.... I am making an impression ...."

21. "On the way here the HERO of Gallipoli took quite a fancy to me, because I could beat him swearing perhaps.... Growing confidential over his liquor and Turkish cigarettes he asked point-blank: 'Didn't I see you at the TWELFTH DAY CEREMONY at the Winter Palace the time the Archbishop lost the golden cross in the river, a few years ago?'... I thought it better to deny the acquaintance and the incident.... I could have easily recalled the ceremony on the Neva, the decorated pavilion on the ice in front of the palace, the procession of church dignitaries in their stiff Byzantine robes and scintillating mitres moving slowly across the road followed by the Grand Dukes and the Emperor, the clear voices of the choir cutting through the frosty air, the ladies of the Court standing near the window and crossing themselves as the Czar stood motionless beneath the gilded and fretted canopy,--I could have recalled it all *... but I swore profanely and declared emphatically that ALL RELIGION WAS A COBWEB AND A SNARE to emancipated minds.... I pretended to get violently MAD about it and told him I would strangle any man who insulted me by accusing me of the most distant relationship with any religion excepting the religion of FREE LOVE.... He laughed like a lion with a sliver in its paw. 'You are* absolutely *the best COUNTERFEIT in circulation that I know of!' he guffawed. 'Well, I'm going to fire Syvorotka and put you in charge of a little FIRING SQUAD when we get to our camping ground at Ekaterinburg!' were his exact words, half whispered, half insinuated and wholly growled across the table in the diner.... With assumed hostility I actually barked: 'The dirtier the deviltry the more diverting!'... He opened his eyes widely like one emerging from a solemn drunk and WINKED knowingly as he shook my hand.... 'You know where Kerensky got his orders to release our fellows, of course,' he whispered. 'I guess you KNOW why he sent* some people *to Ekaterinburg a couple of days before the Czecho-Slovaks are scheduled to* take it, and I guess you know too how it happened that so many MOTOR TRUCKS came all the way from Archangel to Ekaterinburg so as to be on hand when a certain Indian officer shows up, the ridiculous ranter raved.... But...."

"... If these lines should ever come to light I want to record right now, in justice to that apparently besotted creature, that I am under unutterable obligations to him for assigning to me the most diabolical piece of brutality that has been conceived during this period of moral leprosy and unrepenting malevolence.... I shall do my work well."

22. Then the following odds and ends appear:

"... The Metropole performer is a Baroness sure enough.... She knows a Syvorotka but declines to give his rank or whereabouts.... She tells me that this place was founded by Count Tatischshev in 1721 ... when Catherine was a baby.... The Monastery of 'Our Lady of Tikhvin' looming up before me is a very graceful compliment to the Mosque of St. Sophia it resembles in so many ways.... fine place to radio from to friends at Odessa ... especially if the NUN has been obeying orders.... Lvov is out of the way, over in the city prison, cooking, where he can't betray the prisoners at Ipatiev's.... When I was alone with my Imperial prisoner I tore the patch off from my shirt sleeve and handed it to him.... 'Sa lettre!' he exclaimed in an undertone.... His manner was exceedingly polite.... 'Ouvrez, lisez,' I advised.... 'Oui, oui, je sais! je sais!' he said softly, 'mais malheureusement cela est impossible!'... 'Soak it in water', I replied.... 'Et vous, monsieur, etes-vous americain ou francais?' he came back.... 'Je suis ne a Paris, mais je suis americain, and if the prisoner has no objection I'd rather speak in English.'... 'That will be delightful,' he said; 'I shall do as you say.'... He ran back to the bathroom. In a moment he returned holding the patch up before him.... 'Ah!' he continued aloud, 'this merely says that the Heir Apparent will make a cruise of the world in a man-of-war; what does that signify?'... 'If you recognize the writing,' I replied, 'you will, doubtless, remember the methods of its author when extending an invitation.'... 'Yes, yes, I see; how clever of you! Had you been a subject of mine I should have made you an ambassador!'... 'That would imply infinite wisdom on my part, Sire! I bowed very humbly.... It made a hit with my prisoner."

This entry follows:

"Alice will give up her wheel chair when the NUN gives the word ... she is worrying about my prisoner's sister, Olga, and her two companions, who insist on offering their services to the poor in the Crimea ... and well she may!... 'Facing the

East,' ***they are likely to travel*** south!... I must get rid of this old valet, Parafine Domino, who makes a nuisance of himself hovering around my prisoner like a hawk.... Gallipoli says he'll get rid of Alice's physician before the TENTS arrive,--substituting a fake doctor from the Red Guard, who'll tell me when the prisoners are fit to travel.... As 'Captain' of this Soviet Guard I am as cold-blooded as Gallipoli before the spies and hangers-on.... 'Captain?'... that title seems to stump the old Russian soldiers,--they claim that there is no such animal.... The Sergeant has suggested that I put the prisoners under a SMALL GUARD when we take them to the Ural District Soviet Court of Workmen.... Nice trap to catch me.... If I agreed to this I'd be in the same category as Denikin or Dutov or Ekhart and be shot by the gang outside by mistake, so as to fulfill the prophecy of my lady of Buckingham.... My answer was to order the guard on the balcony to keep their guns pointed at the prisoners whenever they appear in the garden ... this will satisfy the eavesdropper in the red brick across the way and scare the wits out of old Parafine, besides giving him something to talk about when we get away.... To satisfy that suspicious Sergeant that there is no Japanese money secreted by the prisoners I have ordered my men to use their bayonets against the walls and ceilings ... even the frame of the bathroom is not to escape!... Gallipoli is growling around that I'm doing my work too damned well to seem reasonable!... The poor boob! His idea of being reasonable ***seems to consist in spreading rumors that the prisoners have been disposed of in a dozen different ways.... When Maria and Tatiana mounted the truck in the yard this confiding swaggerer started the gossip that they were being loaded up to be taken out of town and shot.... Now I am told by some of the excited guard that that report is TRUE because they heard some one in the attic of the red brick yelling:*** 'The baggage is at the station!'...

"When I asked them what we wanted with 'BAGGAGE' they went away growling that I wasn't playing fair!... To my somber-robed lady of Buckingham, who seems to have deserted me, as well as the slender guard at the Huis ten Bosch, as well as those at the Wilhelmstrasse and Odessa, who are part of this 'BAGGAGE,' my guard's agitation will assume the humorous character of unconscious prophecy.... Suspicion is in the air!... This undisciplined gang of cutthroats under that half-baked Sergeant are demanding HOSTAGES from me ***for*** my ***conduct of*** *this business ... they want 'the Grand Dutchess Olga,' her two companions, and FIFTY other women!... AT LAST!... the* planes are buzzing in the sky.... The Ikon of Holy Nicholas is being wrapped up.... The NUN has copies of the letters to Oldenburg and Gendrikov.... It's time to say to my prisoner: Come with ME to the U.D.S. of W.A.R.A.D.'.... If he has the code from Odessa he will ask: 'Are you taking me to be shot?'... 'RUNMOBS'.... I'll have the guard go through his pockets to find the letters that'll turn him over to my 'vengeance' ... then for Ekhart's tunnel and OBLIVION!"

23. Then this entry follows. It seems to be sufficiently circumstantial to justify its reproduction here:

"Murder, like jealousy, in this country is a disease," begins the narrative. "My part in this international murder will paralyze the politician and mystify the sober mind of intelligent belief.... History will not be satisfied, however, without a VICTIM, and I must furnish a victim that will satisfy the mob outside!... The Order has been given.... There are celebrations among the banditti.... there are moistened eyes among many peasants; there are strong men and gallant men among the gang out yonder whose very looks betray the HATRED they entertain for the suspected executioner *of their former ruler and his excited family.... They fear, they try to avoid me; and I can see in their looks that, given a favorable opportunity, they* will hang me to the highest electric wire pole in the city!...

"I am not so certain, though, that EVERYONE outside will accept my theatric 'slaughter' as the Gospel truth.

"Diagonally across the way there has been a Red Cross nurse eternally peeking through her window in this direction.... If we go out into the courtyard she can see us plainly behind the other buildings, for there is nothing to obstruct her vision.... and she seems mighty anxious to keep tab on all proceedings in the yard.... I have tried to figure out a resemblance between this nurse and the capricious Metropole Baroness, but the nurse seems *much older.... Perhaps she is disguised.... If she ever reveals her identity she will remember me as the man who tipped* my *cap to her after posting the two sentries in front of the palisade between the telephone poles and the British Consulate.... If she remembers me she will also recall the drillings I gave my awkward squad for the few days I kept them parading after my prisoners in the yard.... and if anything happens to me she will KNOW that I did my job well up to the minute I write this.... In a few hours more the future political history of the world may be changed forever.... To blot out* seven *lives is all....* Dokonchet the Romanoffs!"

23. This entry follows:

"To satisfy the mob I had to perform a very unpleasant duty.... I use the word duty advisedly, remembering the instructions I committed to memory in the underground office of the Wilhelmstrasse .... Knowing that I am continually WATCHED and spied upon, not only by that nurse in the window over there, but by a number of crazed lunatics in uniform, I was compelled to treat a very pretty Princess shamefully.... News was spread yesterday that Japan had loaned Siberia $250,000,000, and the mob was clamoring for the jewels of the prisoners. This unoffending Princess--this girl, hardly more than seventeen--was holding a conversation in French with her brother Alexis, a little lad of fourteen, in the courtyard. The boy was pale and emaciated from abuse, solitude and confinement. The Princess, a radiant beauty under this hot July sun, was trying to cheer Alexis up. Her gown was badly soiled and of a simple soft material that seemed to accentuate her modest resignation and glorify her courageous cheerfulness in gloom. Her three older sisters, in gowns that spoke of yesterdays, were walking moodily down the path, when a crowd of ruffians burst by the sentries, tore through the doors, and dashed into the yard in the direction of the startled girls.... Taking in the situation quickly, I raised my voice and began swearing like a demon, and prancing around like a skberny *madman.... Then rushing up to Tatiana I TORE FROM HER EARS the jewels that had descended from her early ancestors and howled: 'Aha! you'll wear those cursed things, will you, when your betters are starving in the gutters! Get back, all of you, into your Ipatiev SEPULCHRE and get me ALL the jewelry in the place or* I'll turn these men loose upon you *in three quarters of an hour!... Soldiers,--* attention!!' *... The mob crawled into line.... 'The next time any of you men come into this yard without any orders,' I said, I'll have you SHOT WITH THESE PEOPLE IN THE MANSION!... Column right!... March!'... I heard them mumbling as they passed the first sentry that the cursed interloping* tovarestch *intended to* keep all the loot!'.... Following Alexis and his sisters into the ex-Emperor's study I laid down the earrings upon the flat-topped desk and apologized for my apparent act of cowardice and cruelty....

"There was pathos in that father's soft and courteous voice as he looked at me and said: 'I understand,--yes, yes, I know. You are right--quite right. My darlings, you must not blame this man.'"

VIII
WHEN ROYALTY FACES DEATH

24. This entry follows:

"I must jot this down now--who knows what may happen?... Reminding the family that I had promised results in three quarters of an hour, I instructed them in the part each one must take.... Alexis appeared to be listlessly unconcerned and sat upon one corner of the large flat-topped desk, swinging his feet indifferently; but when I started for the door he sprang to attention like a well-trained soldier and awaited the results.... Going to the door fronting in the main street, I called the sentry and ordered him to CALL OUT THE GUARD.... Shortly my selected guard appeared....

"I conducted them through the dining room and told them to help themselves.... Then we roamed through the living rooms, the boudoirs, straight through to the washing room and bath; then back through the oblong archway into the little square room beyond the study, where I halted them and said: 'Men, these women will die before they'll tell us where the treasure is at present. The OLD MAN and WOMAN seem utterly indifferent to their fate; we can get nothing *out of them. Now, what do you say to giving them a night to think the matter over before we* line them up? We may get more by waiting than by closing their mouths FOREVER....'

"'Not another day!' said one of the men whom I had all along suspected of being suspicious *of MY conduct.... 'What say the rest of you?' I asked.... 'Well,' droned the most courageous of them, with a hangdog expression, 'we might give them until midnight.'... 'Very well,' I snapped viciously, I'LL PUT OFF THE EXECUTION till that hour; then if they don't disgorge I'll kill every one of them* myself!'... 'Not so fast, comrade!' returned the rebellious one; as a member of the guard I believe I'll keep you company .'

"... I knew better than to object.... That man is a cutthroat beyond redemption and will hesitate at nothing to satisfy his lust.... That'll be fine,' I rejoined; 'YOU STAY WITH ME; the rest of the men are dismissed!'... when the men disappeared I made a run and jump at my diabolical 'comrade' and struck him squarely on the nose. Then I smashed him on the mouth, and, with a down drive of my left, I bored into the pit of his stomach and sent him sprawling on the carpet, where he BLED as profusely as a corn-fed bull.... This blood was exactly what I wanted, and in my anxiety to make a good job of it I kicked him several times in the face until he lay there, motionless and senseless, bleeding from every gash.... In the joy of giving this remorseless bully what he needed to overcome his pride I OVERLOOKED ENTIRELY THE PROPRIETY OF MAKING HIM BLEED IN ALL THE OTHER ROOMS.... This little oversight may cost me a well-earned reputation for efficient management I have hitherto enjoyed among many great men of our times, if the omission be detected by some enterprising commission, some journalist or SERVICE man who will certainly check up my report if I leave this place alive...."

25. This entry follows:

"It was a long wait till midnight when the mob outside expected to be invited to a division of the spoils.... but my plans were taking shape gradually as the moments slipped away.... In this isolated, though nicely furnished and elegant two-story dwelling, I got closer to the heart of my celebrated prisoner and his family than any other man alive.... In the few hours left to us before the time set for their 'execution'--in these evening shadows of July, 1918,--we have been discussing the effect of THEIR SACRIFICE upon the history of the world.... I put this down from memory:

"'It is understood already in certain chancellories,' my prisoner significantly replied, 'how my execution will be publicly accounted for.... Each Ministry will appoint a Commission, suggested by the Crown, to investigate and publish its own report.... The report published will be given out under the name of a Naval or Military Commission to impart an official sanction to the supposed inquiry and support the authenticity of the document agreed upon.... Naturally these prearranged reports will vary so as to satisfy the state of mind in each particular country.'... 'If regicides are so easily arranged,' I observed cautiously, 'perhaps the duration of this

"Revolution" is also definitely determined?'... There'll be a period of revolution and distress,' my prisoner remarked, 'before our country settles down to industry and contentment. But the desire of "self-determination" will mislead the unfortunate and cause them to embrace a tyranny of the most cruel and selfish type. This will last for a time until gluttony destroys itself, as all excesses do. When the country is dismembered by the activities of rival greeds, my poor and honest peasants will turn upon their masters and restore this nation's power. They need but education to accomplish glorious results. They will obtain this education while they suffer and evolve a science of self-government while learning to govern themselves. It may seem strange to others when I say so; but not one of my whole family is covetous of the Imperial Crown. We prefer peace and liberty to all the pomp and penalties of Royal isolation from the rest of men and women in the world. Royalty means SLAVERY of the most humiliating form. The boy or girl that is doomed to Royal birth steps into a prison with the first breath he breathes.... Take my own case; I longed to get out and play rough-and-tumble with the boys I saw staring at me in the streets. But I was taught by my English tutor, Heath, that it would be lowering my dignity to associate with those fine young boys. My "dignity" was placed in a strait-jacket and, in a namby-pamby way, I was taught to play ALONE. I had cousins scattered over Europe who took their lot more happily than I; but even they regretted the mocking barriers that laid down a barrage between us and the more fortunate chaps outside,--outside, they enjoyed FREEDOM,--within, we were ALL prisoners in our little cells of etiquette and traditionary bondage. At fifteen I was dragged away to the Military Academy at Petrograd[3] and made to listen to old Danilovich until I actually hated the very name of war. I resolved at that time to inaugurate some means to get rid of such senseless waste of life if intrusted with the power. The Hague was my interpretation of what should constitute a proper exercise of international obligation. You realize, of course, the precarious state of Russia in a military sense,--while force was indispensable to hold us all together from within, it always exposed our weakness when directed toward external issues. I could not map out my own general education, even; forced by the traditions of my family I was placed in charge of the Holy Synod and taught by Pobedonostzev to regard myself as the source of SPIRITUAL POWER and instructed to regard an unortho-

---

3   Nicholas used "Petrograd," not the German nomenclature.

dox opinion as a transportation offense. Now, while I reverence profoundly the sacred tenets of my holy religion, I regard religious freedom as indispensable to the dignity of spiritual belief. For that reason I made that reformation in 1905. As I grew up I rebelled against my intolerable confinement,--I went out among the PEOPLE and TALKED WITH THEM. They were friendly in most instances and gave me very good advice. I did not need a bodyguard to go about. I was as safe among the people as I would be in the Winter Palace. Often have I walked to the hotels alone to call on some particular friend without any thought of fear. Nor was it necessary,--I liked the people as genuinely as I believe they respected me. I learned their hunger for land by going around; and it was on that account that I projected and completed our Siberian Railways so as to give our people the coveted opportunity and an outlet to the markets of the world. Given an opportunity to accumulate and prosper, men will hesitate about going to war unless THEY ARE MISLED. I saw such an opportunity in international trade. I visited the Orient, extensively investigating the commercial field in that direction. It was a mighty task, necessitating a reference to others who should have been as much interested in the accomplishment as I was myself. Their mistakes have made me quite unhappy and there has always been CONTENTION between my Ministers and myself. If Witte had kept his hands off when Count Solsky got after the plotting school teachers and rebellious students, the propaganda against my reign which has honeycombed the Empire with sedition might have been checked in time to prevent this dissolution,--for it is more than a "revolution." It is idealism run amuck. France, England, the people of America, have been duped by the intelligentia--the Kadets--who never seemed to realize that in order to hold this Empire together not only FORCE but SUPERSTITION was required,--'si mundus vult decipi decipiatur,' it is the only principle that will hold unorganized ignorance in disciplinary subjection to orderly and regulated progress; and without this discipline the ARMY, or the power that holds this incongruous Nation together, will dissolve, as you may now see, while the whole Empire will fly to pieces. My strong Ministers were too physical and myopic to look beyond their noses. They were afraid to seem afraid of truth,--and they even accused me of plotting with Kazantsev and Feodorov against the life of my Minister of Finance,--always excuses for fomenting discontent! They never seemed to realize that the HAPPINESS of the PEOPLE meant the SECURITY of the CROWN. As a matter of fact the only loyal supporters I ever had around me were my wife and family besides a few others in the service of the State. When I announced my war aims on the Pacific for the benefit of my people my leading Minister had the audacity to obtrude upon my privacy at Tsarskoye Selo and demand that I withdraw the manifesto. This piece of impudence cost me the decision in that war. That magniloquent Minister, with his versatile Irish amanuensis, not only turned my mother against me, but he had the temerity to demand that I dismiss my best agent, Azeff, who alone kept me advised of the machinations of the Social Revolutionists, who, in turn, accused me of murdering my uncle Sergius--the greatest theologian of the age. As I recall the time, now, I am, of course, convinced that the only real friend *I had among those Social Revolutionists was BURTZEV,--but I understood him too late!'... My prisoner spoke regretfully. His voice was soft and courteous, breaking at times into the altisonance of the tragic muse. He does not think that any act of his can be wrong; the mere fact that HE ran counter to accepted standards divests, in his mind, the act itself of turpitude. That seems to be the way he looked upon his former Eastern encroachments. That's the way he justified his subterranean deals with the KAISER; and he even goes so far as to assert that* 'if the Vyborg-Bjoerkesund treaty had not been denounced the present war would not have happened.' He speaks of this a little passionately, scorning the very memory of Count Witte for 'questioning the morality of that arrangement.' That great Minister my prisoner refers to as 'an uncouth bully who bellowed like a mad bull.' In this respect it is my impression that the ex-Empress indorses his state of mind. What he likes she will place in the superlative; what he merely hates, she *elevates to positive abhorrence. In this way she seems to flatter his decisions, which makes him smile quite indulgently at her, and hold her ascendency over his apparently veering mind. I can notice this in so many little things: She oozes delicate flattery and he likes it; she plays upon his* prejudices, and he seems to have a lot of them submerged beneath his inalienable urbanity and instinctive grace of manner that even this misery and abysmal gloom have not relieved of polish. Beneath it all I get the impression that he is very much in love with every member of his family.... that he would like to be alone *with 'Alice,' whom he addresses as 'my darling' and experiences a shell-shock if she stubs her toe. His final words are: 'Now it is ALL*

OVER and I WILL WELCOME THE OBLIVION that will release us all from the memory of our devoted bondage!'... While my prisoner conversed Alexis assisted his stately mother and his four beautiful sisters while putting on their superannuated wraps.... One by one they filed out the door leading into the open yard.... My prisoner stood up and stretched himself.... He was about to resume his seat when the report of a revolver resounded in our ears.... The brute on the floor, wallowing in his blood, was raised upon his elbows and firing recklessly.... After he had fired six rounds without apparent injury I drew my own revolver and fired deliberately INTO THE WALL.... The fellow slunk back to silence.... My prisoner and I followed the ladies out into the night, forgetting a jewel or two in our leisurely departure.... Out in the open WE DESCENDED into the old abandoned tunnel that formerly led from Ipatievs to the medical office of a foreign consulate a thousand feet away...."

IX
WHAT IS LEARNED IN A SECRET TUNNEL

26. The next entry is mystifying:

"We are between the devil and the deep sea!... which gives me time to write.... The beastly tunnel has caved in midway in our passage.... It seems, from the roar overhead, that we are somewhere beneath the railroad tracks. Yet there must be a vent somewhere, as there seems to be a draft of air through this passage.... The family are congregated off to the right, in a kind of stoping where the dirt has been removed, leaving a small room like one meets with in the Gogebic iron mines in Wisconsin and Michigan, back in the United States.... Our little electric bull's-eyes come in handy just now.... With my bull's-eye propped up on a sand-encrusted box I am noting down some things that must not be forgotten.... While trying to find a passageway out of this hole in the ground we gyrated back and forth for the last two or three hours until the women became exhausted.... Then my 'prisoner' and I returned to the mouth of the entrance. There we heard a horrible row between the unruly brute we left on the floor and his wild-eyed fellow conspirators.... They accused him of DOUBLE-CROSSING THEM and making away with the treasure that they insisted should be theirs!

"... He insisted that there was NO treasure EXCEPT the JEWEL he apparently was exhibiting.... We could hear, quite distinctly, a sullen voice saying: 'I do not believe you; you are trying to steal the whole of it!... We'll give you ten minutes to produce ALL you have hid away, and if you don't do it, we'll fill your body so full of lead that your rotten carcass won't float in the Kolunda.'... The culprit replied: 'Let me explain. You remember that I was suspecting that interloper *when I insisted on watching him; well, my suspicions were correct,--he was a TRAITOR to our cause. He was planning to steal away with his precious gang when I covered them with my pistol. Then when I had the drop on them I made them open all of their trunks and boxes. Nothing was found. I felt sure they were holding out on me, so I took a shot at the kid. The interloper made a dive at me. I knocked him down with that chair there.... then in my rage I emptied my pistol into the hearts of the whole gang.... that's all there's to it.'...* 'He's lying!' 'Traitor!' 'Betrayer!' 'Down with the thief!' *flew back and forth from one to another above our heads.... Then in a more subdued voice we heard 'Hist!* Silence! Some one is coming!' A moment later I heard distinctly the unmistakable growl of my hero of Gallipoli overhead demanding, 'WHAT HAVE YOU CUTTHROATS DONE WITH OUR PRISONERS?' ... There was a silence *that could be felt.... None offered an explanation that I could hear.... 'Why don't you answer?' thundered Gallipoli.... There was an unmistakable murmur.... 'Don't YOU try to slide out of this, you COWARD! I'll hold* every one *of you responsible for this!* Where's my lieutenant?'... He means ME....

"'Out in the yard,' I heard one of them reply.... 'Go and tell him to report here AT ONCE!'... Poor devil! the humor of this whole situation is displayed in the tragic possibilities of criminal greed when crooks fall out!... 'Where are the others?' my Gallipoli hero demanded.... I heard no answer.... 'DO YOU HEAR ME?'... still no audible answer.... 'Crack!'.... the report of a revolver, then a scuffling and 'stand back! *Another move and I'll blow you ALL to HELL,--*line up there!.... Now I order you to explain the whereabouts of the PRISONERS.'

"... We could hear a voice boasting: 'Did you see that BLOOD in yonder? Well, that is our answer. We were suspicious of that Lieutenant of yours so we took the matter into our own hands.'... 'WHO DID THE KILLING?'... 'The Sergeant.'... 'And what did he DO with the bodies?'... 'Threw them into the well!'... 'The devil! you'll have to fish them out again!'... Then there was a long silence.... Finally we heard: 'Here, Sergeant!' from HE of Gallipoli; 'when will my lieutenant report?'... 'The Captain said to present his compliments and say that he is temporarily detained.'... My 'prisoner' poked me in the ribs impulsively and smiled.... 'Where are the BODIES?'... 'Burned!' said the Sergeant. 'WHAT?'... 'BURNED UP?... 'Who burned them?'... 'I did, Sir.'... 'Didn't throw them in the well?'... 'No, Sir.'... 'Well, I'll be damned!... FALL IN! Unless those prisoners are produced I'll court-martial every one of you!'

"... We could hear the measured tread of a squad overhead tramping until the thump, thump, thumping sank into a faint indistinct vibration which was caught up by the beating of our hearts and the throbbing of our fascinated and incredulous ears.... 'Well!' ejaculated my amused 'prisoner'; 'It'll be exceedingly interesting to read the future accounts of my double execution. I am sure my family will read it with greater interest than they've ever manifested in any of London's or Gorky's fanciful novels!'... 'I assume that you will not be surprised to learn that you have some mighty good friends in that crowd outside,' I ventured.... 'Oh, not at all,' my prisoner returned, 'and I venture to say that your friend from Gallipoli will find it convenient to contribute to the general misunderstanding and confusion by allowing the suspected executioners to air their conflicting explanations of my disappearance.'

"'We haven't disappeared yet, my friend!' I grumbled, as we turned back in the direction of our underground camp.... 'If we had some shovels it would solve the problem; but the way we're fixed it looks like a case of starvation or surrender for the whole of us,--we can't stay down here indefinitely!'... 'Patience, courage, my friend,' my 'prisoner' replied whole-heartedly; 'this is the first time in my life I have been absolutely alone, the first moment in our lives we have been positively FREE!'... He took a few swift steps and swung around gracefully, like a figure in a dance.... 'I love the mazurka!' he exclaimed!... 'I'd like to have a real pillow fight again with the children!... We used to have such fun!... It was about the only time my wife would ever smile!... I used to tell her that she reminded me of the sad goddesses that stood on the dull red cornices of my Winter Palace looking coldly into space during any of the Court ceremonies.... Really that was true,--a woman like my wife, in a manteau de cour, *a head flaming with the rays of her kokoshnik and supported by that long white veil, DOES resemble an icicle in the Winter Palace!... But when we are* alone!... the Zaritsa is a motherly MOTHER!... You'll see.... We have always loved simplicity.... This is our chance.... I never did like the late suppers and high life indulged in by some of my relations.... My greatest dissipation was at the Marinsky when we'd sup between acts and go straight home to bed.... Grand Duke Alexis never wanted to go to bed.... After the theatre he was always primed for another party out at the Islands.... Our motto has always been, "Early to bed and early to rise."... Had to.... At work early after breakfast till eleven ... luncheon ... to work again at half past twelve until dinner ... back to work until very late at night.... NOW we are hearing of our misguided workmen and soldiers *attempting to run the country on SIX HOURS WORK A DAY!... That would be delightful if they would only devote the remaining hours to recreation and STUDY.'... My 'prisoner' seemed positively* boyish....

"His voice was in pleasant contrast to the shrill staccato accents I had heard in that gloomy underground room of the Foreign Office at Berlin.... I could see at a glance that his present attitude was not a pose,--his simplicity, like his courage and democracy, was GENUINE.... It explains the reason for his composure at THIS VERY MINUTE when a less courageous man would be excitedly running around in circles and making my life miserable by bemoaning our ill luck.... To show the mo-rale *of this family of cave dwellers I'll record this incident: 'Be careful about those electric lamps,' I requested of the ladies. 'If they give out we'll be in dark-ness.' ... 'Then we'll use our hands and dig ourselves out to daylight!' exclaimed Maria.... 'WHY can't we start doing THAT NOW?' exclaimed Tatiana.... 'Come on!' chorused Alexis and his four sisters as they fell to and are now pawing the dirt away from the embankment that impedes our escape.... I'll have to supervise that work a little, for if these girls continue to pile back the dirt the way they are doing it they may stop up the passage both ways and* bury us all alive...."

X
ROMANCE IN SIGHT OF DEATH

28. The next page of the diary is badly blurred and torn, but the following can be made out:

"We are all about played out.... The boy is exhausted and lying over in a little excavation upon his sisters' wraps, his fingers bleeding and one eye blinded with the sand.... The passageway behind us is almost closed up.... In front of us we have hit a solid wall.... The exhausted mother is binding her boy's hands with a portion of her petticoat.... As she kneels there, with the faint flicker of a light falling on her finely chiseled profile, she resembles Botticelli's magnificent ***Madonna in the Uffizi Gallery at Florence.... The picture is completed by the dark background and the solicitous attitude of the girls as they cluster around the sufferer.... With a little imagination one can delineate the jeweled crown which the two girlish angels are holding above her head.... Pathos, resignation and a sort of recreating FAITH are painted against that threatening wall and overhanging dirt.... If that should fall WE ARE ALL BOUND TO SUFFOCATE before any help can come.... My 'prisoner' is not a bit discouraged, however.... He is using his jackknife against the concrete wall with great patience and whistling softly and slowly an air from 'The Blessing of the Waters.'... WATER!... I know those girls are CHOKING for a drink as I have been for the last ten hours myself.... Still, not one of them has murmured at our grief and Anastasie has become quite chummy in pretending to cheer ME up.... Aristocracy or Royalty, even, with Democracy in a tunnel, makes us ALL of one size! Under certain conditions a man of my education and family connections MIGHT be privileged to forget the veiled lady*** *of Buckingham and accept these endearing little attentions with some guarantee of hope.... But WHAT IF WE ALL ARE BURIED HERE like the happy families of Herculaneum and Pompeii?... Future inquisitive scientists may find this diary with our* bones *and classify us as a species of an extinct Tartar tribe!... The wall my prisoner is gouging out* seems to be getting wet...."

29. Then there follows the entry:

"Water has burst through the hole my prisoner has been making in that wall!..."

30. The next entry has been evidently water-soaked and is entirely blotted out.

31. This entry seems sufficiently distinct to make out what the writer has been through:

"I tried in the foregoing to jot down enough of what was happening to enable anyone who would find our bodies to make out how we had died.... What I forgot to record in the excitement I'll put down now.... When the wall caved in and the water burst down upon us it seemed that we would soon be drowned alive.... The small hole in the wall had allowed enough water to filter through at first to slake our thirst and make us all quite happy.... But gradually the ground beneath us became damp and sticky and the blue mud clung to our shoes like glue until we could hardly move.... The little air that crept in with the water, though, was a positive blessing to us all.... We should have stifled.... Finally the water ceased and our hearts began to sink....

"... It was Maria who brought on the FLOOD I have learned today.... With a stone she found uncovered by the filtering from the little opening she began pounding against the wall.... Suddenly the wall bulged inward.... There was a swish, and a roar, and a deadening GUSH,--and then a RUSHING FLOOD tore open the side of the wall and burst like a torrent into our muddy, narrow cell. Higher and higher it mounted, enveloping us to our arm pits.... My 'prisoner' moved calmly over to the stately woman, who was holding up the boy, and patted her gently on the head. 'It will be all right, darling,' he said.... Then he kissed all his children and impulsively dashed in the direction of the cataract.

"... Struggling hard against the flood he worked his way nearer and nearer toward the broken curbing and finally DOVE through the waterspout and clung grimly to the wall.... For a moment his body seemed to tremble.... Then with a supreme effort he pulled his body into the opening and for a moment checked the flood.... It seemed like a gallant sacrifice.... at the same time.... the girl, Maria, waded back toward the opening that was NOW completely SEALED BY THE STICKY CLAY and began to tear frantically at the bank....

"Little by little she seemed to make headway.... But it appeared like an eternity,--and I felt certain that the man in the wall using his body as a plug must presently give up the ghost and be hurled back into our cell.... I then noticed the water around us DROP quickly, and, turning in the direction of Maria I saw her body being caught up by the current and sucked painfully forward into the opening her delicate hands had made.... It was too horrible to endure!... Now, while there is no blood of martyrs in my veins, and while I had PROMISED the sombre figure in Berlin TO DO A CERTAIN THING which a martyr impulse might prevent if I tried to be a hero in this instance, I simply could not look at that girl's struggles without going to her rescue no matter what it cost...."

32. The following then appears:

"I have no recollection of what happened after I grasped Maria by the feet.... All I remember is that I felt myself being dragged along after her through a blinding sheet of muddy, gritty substance, head foremost like a drowning man.... I imagined myself in mid-ocean clinging to some broken shaft after my vessel had been torpedoed, and I clung to those slender ankles as the only hope of life!... When I did recover there was Maria bending over me and vigorously see-sawing my arms back and forth in an effort to resuscitate me.... If ever there were an excuse for the chivalry of the Middle Ages it must have crept out of those dark moments when some puissant knight opened his tired eyelids upon a vision such as I then beheld!... But there was no time for Don Quixoting in that damp and muddy tunnel.... We noticed that the waters neither rose nor fell.... So we plowed our way back to the other members of our party as speedily as we could.... On arriving at the wall again we found my 'prisoner' lying propped up against a large slab of concrete and breathing heavily while he held the Empress' hand and essayed a feeble smile...."

33. The following entry seems to dovetail in:

"The walls of this old cistern promise very little assurance for our escape.... Still the cistern has its uses in circumstances like these.... We KNOW, at least, that some kind of human beings are not beyond our voices if we decide to call for help.... But WHAT KIND of help?... That is the question.... Last night, as I stood on the floor of the cistern I heard an amusing conversation.... A voice overhead was growling; 'I'm as certain as I'm alive that the loan of $250,000,000 has been made by Japan to those fiends who have escaped,--and I KNOW they have the GOLD, for why have those trucks disappeared?... so it is worth while to keep up this revolution until we get our hands on some of it if we have to follow them all the way to Vladivostok.'... 'That rumor has been floating around for the past week,' another bass voice grumbled, 'and I'm inclined to think it is all a game of bunko to divert attention from the pile of 600,000,000 the gang have smuggled into Omsk.'... 'Nonsense,' grunted the other; 'haven't we a thousand eyes at Harbin who know about the Chinese Eastern deal?'... 'Well, the only thing to do is to keep this hell in a constant bubble until we get the stuff at Omsk or the coin Japan has sent to this CREMATED FAMILY here!'...

"... 'Cremated, Ha! Ha!... why, did you notice those stoves in the house?... They're not big enough to burn up a good-sized dog!... My judgment tells me that that whole squad of double-crossers are in league with that skunk of a "Captain" who pretended to be a friend of Comrade Trotsky.'... 'Well, we made a mistake when we endorsed that BURNING lie,--we are ALL in for it NOW, and the only way to get out of it is to STAY IN IT and lie it out to the end--'.... 'UNLESS--' 'Unless what?'... 'Unless the Lett who pretended to do the killing is taken out and SHOT!'... 'Oh, give him a little more rope and he'll hang himself!'... When I related this conversation to my 'prisoner' he was very much amused.... 'This is a real adventure!' he smiled. 'We're like Tennyson's Light Brigade, with cannons in front, and cannons behind us and brigands on every side of us, thirsting for our blood,--these fellows are certainly not Russians!'..."

34. Then we have this entry:

"I have noticed all day that the family is gradually succumbing to the ravages of hunger and thirst.... If we call for help it will mean a FIRING SQUAD for sure.... The criminal crew who have already reported our death will HAVE to KILL us to make good their boast.... So we must stay here and silently watch one another collapse from day to day....

"... My prisoner says he is willing to give himself up if his death will enable the rest of us to escape.... The girls will not listen to such a proposition,--they are all agreed that they would rather organize themselves into a little platoon and FIGHT IT OUT if we can ever get out of this cistern.... It indicates a mighty good spirit,-- but that gang outside would have us strung up in the twinkling of an eye....

"... I KNOW that Marie expects ME to do something from the inquiring way she gazes in my eyes.... She says nothing, but any man of spirit who looks into such clear, unflinching eyes under conditions such as these, will understand instinctively what is written in their suggestive depths!... They literally SHAME me for the little I can do.... Some lounge lizards may speculate on the nature of the sentiments this grateful princess will reveal if I display sufficient ingenuity to save us all from this slowly approaching DEATH!... How dramatic!... How absurd!

"... I have lately laughed at those Italian poets who bewail the isolation of their Lauras, yet, recalling my Lady Buckingham's repeated rescues, I begin to recognize a reason for the existence of that poetic fervor which agitates the artistic heart when either its safety or its vanity is at stake.".....

35. This entry offers a little encouragement:

"There is no such thing as physical exhaustion.... Hunger and thirst may weight us down, but with the right kind of inspiration a man can do miraculous things.... I began rolling up balls of mud from the tunnel and carrying them into the cistern until my tongue hung out of my mouth.... With those balls I started making a wind- ing stairway around the wall of this cistern until I had a dozen steps completed ... then the girls began making the balls and bringing them in to me like muddy little hod-carriers.... My masonry took on proportions as the minutes dragged by.... Fi- nally we have a stairway four feet wide and extending from the bottom to within four feet of the top as I write these lines with the girls sitting a few steps below me in the slowly hardening clay.... We can all hear plainly the tramping of feet on the planking overhead.... It is a kind of shuffling one hears when seated somewhere beneath the dancers in a ballroom, and it may mean that we are headed directly toward the LION'S DEN.".....

36. In this entry the Emperor speaks of Rasputin, spooks and Jews:

"It became dark and spooky when our lights gave out.... and while we sat hud- dled together the subject of 'ghosts' came up.... 'Ghosts!' the 'prisoner' almost snarled; 'that reminds me of the Jewish propaganda against my Government.... There was hardly a Yiddish banker in the world who did not accuse ME personally of inspiring Sheglovitov to have the Jews executed for ritualistic murder; and I am sure their influence will be very strong with certain statesmen and opportunists to have my Empire dismembered when the time comes to settle the terms of peace, as poor Nilus predicted.... I wish I could show you a letter I received from a Jewish banker in New York threatening to kill my loan in America and have our existing treaties denounced unless I complied with certain Jewish demands.... I did not think it possible and ignored the letter, of course.... You may judge of my astonishment when the Jew's threat was made good by the American Government doing precisely what the threat implied.... These people have been persistent in accusing ME of having communication with the spirits *and of engaging in all sorts of* magic, like the infamous Papus; well, if that be so let me exercise my gifts to prophesy that the denationalized Jews will attempt to hereafter enthrone themselves as MASTERS of the civilized world by their mastery of its amusements, its money, its POLITICS and its industry,--and you will find them demanding and RECEIVING special privileges in many countries where, at present, they are suspected and abhorred.... I have not the slightest doubt but that Kerensky will be succeeded by some Jewish politician within a little while--and they will blacken his reputation as they have tried to blacken mine.... the methods may be different but the result will be none the less effectual.... Only the other day, I might say, WHEN WE WERE LEAVING TUMEN, a rabble of Yiddish suttlers *began* yelling at ME: "Rasputin! Rasputin! where is your Rasputin!" ... *Now Grisha Rasputin was a friend of the Metropolitan Archbishop of Protopopov. He was seeking to redeem the reputation of a horse-stealing father if I remember right--'He was a friend of Stuermer, Niki, not a friend to you,' interrupted the ex-Empress... 'You are right, darling,' returned the 'prisoner,' 'quite right, I know.'... 'What kind of a mountebank was RASPUTIN?' I asked to feel my 'prisoner' out.... 'He was a worthless* rasputnik *at best,' the fallen Emperor answered.... And you think the Jews are responsible for your reported attachment to him?' I asked.... 'Undoubtedly,' he said bitterly with a sigh of resignation.... 'When we were being taken to the boat at Tobolsk did they not make faces at me and Alice and flout me with their cries: "Take him to the Criminal Court and let him read the record of his libertine, Rasputin! Let his Barnabas teach him how to sin for the joy of gaining absolution!"... How little do those enfranchised Jews understand the meaning of forgiveness!' lamented the ex-Czar.... 'May I ask your actual estimate of creatures like Rasputin?' I ventured.... 'Our Rasputin was a hardened criminal beyond a doubt until his conversion by Father Zaborovsky, the good Rector at the Theological Academy at Tomsk,' the ex-Czar replied.... 'He would have made an excellent subject for investigation by Lombroso, by Havelock Ellis or other eminent criminologists ... but I believed the man was sincere in his repentance and accepted him as a sort of text for other sinners to point a way toward regeneration.... The higher Rasputin rose, the greater his fame became, the more impressive would be his textual example to other aspiring souls,--even a criminal should not be denied the consolation of hope where crime is the result of ignorance or misdirected patriotism.... If I sinned in pardoning a sinner then sin must be an unpardonable crime!... Nathan treated David as I treated Rasputin, although both were guilty of the same offense.... He was grossly illiterate,--the only schooling he ever got was in the Monastery Abalaksky and what he acquired from the lips of monks while making his rounds as a barefoot pilgrim from place to place.... His claims of having* visions I ascribed to his empty stomach, although others gave credence to the nonsense.... Alice at first abhorred him; finally she began to regard him as a rare specimen in self-hypnosis who was worth studying to learn how far the fascinations of self-delusion were capable of deluding and swaying stronger wills and more cultivated minds.... We both learned, by observing him, that an ignorant mujik, like an egotistical Minister, if granted the semblance of authority for any length of time, will demoralize the finest organization in the world.... That was the lesson both Alice and I acquired from Rasputin.... And I am accepting Rasputin as a standard to estimate what will happen when men of his type and origin attempt the government of the world.... Without education, with no experience in governing even the smallest unit of society, unfamiliar with the trend of history, ignorant of military and commercial strategy, building their philosophy of life and their science of administration upon some isolated text, they will overturn the whole structure of civilization by arrogating to themselves the supernatural privileges and persuasiveness of the Voice of God!... The prospects are not inviting.... There are Rasputins in all the chancellories of Europe.... You have them in North and South America,--some educated, others like Marat and Danton, while some are simple Cagliostros who deceive the people and themselves.... If they were only Gideons instead of Joshuas their strategy might be reassuring,--but they are merely Rasputins and Papuses, after all!... Against all laws of nature they will try to triumph by commanding the heavenly and mundane bodies to stand still until they readjust the motions of civilized society to some dissolving and ruinous invention of emotional insanity where everything runs wild!'"

XI
THE INVISIBLE DIPLOMAT APPEARS

37. This entry is mystifying:

"Last night I waited until there was not a sound overhead.... I knew it would be taking chances--but I HAD TO GET WATER.... We could no longer survive on MUD!... I began pushing against the planking overhead to see if there was anywhere an opening, but every plank I pressed against seemed as solid as a stone sidewalk.... Finally I began thumping with my clenched fist ... and this brought on the fracas.... I heard a heavy pair of feet bounding on the floor directly above my head.... Then there was a scraping and a sound like the tearing up of carpets.... Presently I heard an iron bolt crack back and the floor above my head began rising slowly until I found myself looking into the muzzle of a Mauser held in the clenched hands of a tall square-faced man with a jaw like a prize fighter....

"... Another pair of hands reached down and caught me by the collar and I was yanked like a squirming spaniel out of my hole into a large oblong room that was only slightly lighted by a blue student lamp upon a small roll-top desk.... Against the wall was a large steel engraving of King George of England, and I could see the Union Jack displayed upon another wall.... There were papers and documents and army tents in piles here and there round the room.... BUT THE IMPRESSION THAT FLASHED UPON ME was not at all reassuring for a man who had made his way into SUCH surroundings directly from the other underground corridor in Berlin!..."

38. Then this entry follows:

"From that very hour I AM STRONGLY FOR THE BRITISH.... I will not attempt to describe that MEAL.... It was all a King in Exile or any of his suite could ask for; and the silent men who prepared it will always be remembered for their discretion and manly hospitality.... Neither of them appeared to KNOW me NOR ANY OF OUR PARTY.... But those gallant fellows are adepts at dissimulation.... I'm certain that the tall, slender and soldierly bearing officer will remember the day we had our STRAWBERRIES at Carlton Terrace, and the slender, willowy Duchess who forgot her fan until he picked it up and brought it to her AT MY TABLE, where she paused for a moment to say to me, 'MY FATHER IS IN LONDON AND WISHES TO SEE YOU BADLY.'... I am certain he remembers what I told her about the Gordons and the Devons in that slaughter at the Somme,--when so few of those brave lads returned!... If we ever meet again I shall thank him for the robes and provisions and motor trucks he furnished to transport us safely rolled up in army tents for many rough miles across the country in the direction of CHANYI LAKE...."

39. We find this entry of the diarist next:

"I have never beheld a more beautiful landscape than the scene before me.... I am writing this on the banks of Altai Lake.... The balsam from the cone-like firs along the gorges surcharges the air with an intoxicating flavor and reflect their inverted gracefulness in the calm waters of the lake.... The mountains sloping up from either side are delineated in the mirroring surface and form an archway for the snow-capped and broken pinnacle that towers above the others like a sentinel brooding in his frosty and eternal isolation.... Far off in the distance I can see the black and white walls of the KATUN GLACIER and know that, throughout this region, gold and silver, as well as lead and copper, most certainly abound.... In our unending tramp today I have discovered many evidences of the presence of zinc and nickel and other minerals lying around.... My 'prisoner' tells me that there are mines already working in the upper part of the Talovsky River and that the copper runs very high in the vicinity of Chudak.... Alice wrote to Princess G---- today at T----.... I am NOT much impressed nor FAVORABLY by the attitude of these natives in the hills.... They seem to be a mongrel mixture of Tartar and Mongolian who are always ready, like the huge ungainly bears we have encountered in our pilgrimage, to grapple and devour one for the mere pleasure of seeing blood!... Maria seems quite interested in these notes,--today she insisted on giving me her impressions of how a NOVEL should be written.... She says that to make a story interesting it should be all movement from the opening line to the final wedding bells.... When I told her that I was writing HISTORY she pouted prettily and remarked: 'I never think of history without wondering WHO subsidized the writer of the misleading fairy tale.'

"... This girl has lived close enough to the source of history to know what PRO-PAGANDA is.... Still, I like her uncomplaining buoyancy of spirits in the trial we are going through.... We are headed SOUTH toward Kuria and Khotan, where arrangements have been made to receive us by some people who know our secret and will respect the rights of ASYLUM in a land where oblivion may mean liberty and love!..."

40. There seems to have been quite a skip in the notations of the diary. Evidently the diarist has become MORE INTERESTED in something else:

"The fact that we have been on FOREIGN SOIL during the last fifteen days has considerably relaxed our nerves.... Aside from the rumor constantly reaching us that the Mongolian mercenaries are in the employ of the Bolsheviki and offered BIG REWARDS for our capture, we have not been disturbed in mind or bodies.... Maria asked me today if I were any relation to CHARLES JAMES FOX, whose oratory she claims to greatly admire.... When I informed her that I had never met this gentleman her eyes grew very big....

"'What ARE you?' she inquired. 'Are you an Englishman, or a Russian,--you CAN NOT BE A GERMAN,--or ARE YOU AN AMERICAN? Oh, I just hope you ARE an AMERICAN!... When I informed her that my ancestors fought beside Kosciusko and Pulaski and that their names might be found on the muster rolls of the First Line Regiment of New York Colony and State, along with the names of Goose Van Schaick and Jeremiah Van Rensselaer, she burst her sides with laughter.... 'What a happy family you must have been!' she rippled. 'When a Fox and a Goose may dwell in peace and amity together there is nothing that is not possible for their race!' "... This quick-witted girl, certainly, BELONGS in the UNITED STATES--the plains of Eastern Turkestan are NO place for her...."

41. There seems to be another skip in the neglected diary. Evidently the scenery has lost all its charms.... He merely notes:

"My 'prisoner' seems VERY MUCH interested in my family connections.... He seems jolly enough about it.... BUT I can see that something is DISTURBING him.... He is very obstinate in little things, lately.... When we get into Cashmere perhaps his mind will be diverted.... He loves the languid charm of scenic beauty nearly as

much as the flattery of his wife.... Anyway, WHAT can I do?... There is a natural-
ness about this whole affair that one simply CAN'T get away from.... Danger has a
generous way of bestowing blessings on the BOLD..."

42. Then we find the following critical entry: "I shall NEVER read 'Lalla Rookh'
again!... The Vale of Cashmere may sound fine in poetry but it FEELS TOUGH beneath one's feet whenever one dismounts.... I might overlook the rough spots easily
enough had not OLGA suddenly interested herself in my ANCESTRY while she
found employment for Maria with her brother, who seems sadly out of breath....
My 'prisoner' has forgotten all about me in the absorbing interest he displays in
what he declares to be EARLY MISSIONARY WORK OF JESUS in these very interesting stretches. It has been no easy matter for me to pilot this party outside the
range of camel caravans and soldiers on their way from the Punjab Valley toward
RAWAL PINDI.... The rattle of our tongas might be heard at any moment and then
our little caravan, disguised as Buddhists, might spend some time in the GUARD-
HOUSE at Murree.... We will not regret the shade and comparative coolness of that
pleasant Summer Resort,--but none of us are longing for any more confinement....
The road from Murree down the valley was gullied by the terrific rain we have
been wading through.... I have never seen a blacker night nor a heavier rain than
we have just come through... We were constantly in fear of the falling of those gi-
gantic boulders that overhung our path behind the swishing trees that clung along
the precipice.... The zigzag road that runs down this slope is like a spiral stair in
crookedness and bumps.... We could catch a glimpse now and again of a light from
the little bungalows that clung to the mountain sides.... But we dare not arouse the
dwellers for many obvious reasons.... Finally we did encounter an abandoned inn or
hut where we camped for the night.... Next morning in a fierce and searching sun
we rambled into a village set upon a wonderful defile in the heart of the mountains,
where we ate our frugal meal.... At night we reached the Jhelum coursing gracefully
over rocky beds and through picturesque gorges that rise into the azure and serene
skies of the Himalayan heavens.... It was a delightful place to camp for the night....
At nine the next morning we had reached the little hamlet strung along the river
bank and known as Tongua.... Here the girls made a number of purchases and we
replenished our commissary for the march before us into mystic dominions of the
LAMA...."

XII
THE FLIGHT TO TIBET

43. Then we get this entry:

"I did not count the number of Hindu castes we encountered at the trading post of Tongua.... there were a hundred, at least, each bearing on his forehead the mani-colored mark of his particular caste,--while the stately Kashmirian in his snowy turban and long white tunic seemed carved out of the frozen snows of the towering mountain sides.... we were offered many cabriolets to assist us on our journey, but one look at one of those backless and circular TABLES between the wheels upon which one must sit like a Turkish mouker with his legs crossed to keep from rolling down the precipice was enough to convince us that the camel route was good enough for us.

"On the tramp to Horis, along the banks of the Jhelum with its wooded mountains on the right and its rocky precipices on the left, we met a number of pilgrims who had religious scruples against taking part in letting blood of any kind of bird or beast or whale.... They had evidently been to their Mecca.... Another thing we discovered that is not generally understood among the unelect.... On the way we came upon a Hindu squatting by the roadside with a pail of rich fresh milk.... Being thirsty I pointed at the pail and asked him for enough to give our party a drink.... The fellow became enraged and informed me that I had defiled his milk by pointing my finger at it.... I said I'd take it all, which was evidently what he wished.

"After we had all drunk our fill I took the half-filled pail, approached the grinning rascal and deliberately dashed the contents in his face!... My 'prisoner' was horrified, but Maria enjoyed it very much.... 'I had one experience in Japan,' my 'prisoner' confided, 'that has taught me never to oppose the local customs of a country no matter how absurd they may seem to others.... At that time one of my party poked fun at the peculiar art displayed in the statue of a Buddha.... The priest became enraged and attempted to split my head open when I was not looking.... Had it not been for my cousin I'm sure I would not be with you today!... You will please me much if you respect the ancient practices of these people.'...

"Then going to the dripping figure he laid a gold louis on the fellow's upturned palm,--HE SEEMED TO KNOW WHAT WAS COMING--which was proof to my mind that there is more in Yogi philosophy than has ever been let out....

"... Frankly, however, I suspect that my 'prisoner's' kindness has only whetted the appetite of that knave.... The way he looks at us would convict him in any court of justice that he meditates our murder...."

44. Then we have this entry:

"I am not at all mistaken in my estimate of that Hindu with the pail of defiled milk.... He is one of the renegade SPIES that hang on the brow of civilization and infest these retreats and mountain gorges in search of easy prey.... There are other POWERS above them that lounge in gilded palaces and seem always interested in the charms of lovely women who may suddenly DISAPPEAR.... I know the brood of vultures from Stamboul to the red lights of New York and the dens of Singapore!... The quicker we get down out of these mountains and into the populated valley on our way to Seranagur the SAFER I will feel.... It is all very pleasant to take a look at this silver ring that encircles the plateau with its eternal snows, to watch the sparkling waterfalls, the gardens and the dimpling lake with its little islands with cottages resting on them and to imagine one's self in the fairyland we used to read about as children,--BUT for a full-grown man, in my position and charged with an important mission, I prefer to be on my way.... There are too many places where one may be accounted for as having fallen down the mountain side in the event of some sudden DISAPPEARANCE!"

45. By the initiated the following entry will not be misunderstood:

"It was an unlucky piece of folly that sent us in this direction halfway round the earth to a destination we could have reached in fifteen days.... On our way to Bombay where arrangements had been made to slip us quietly across the Peninsula and on to our permanent retreat, we were confronted with the information that people of my prisoner's nationality were leaving *Bombay* by request,--and hence our unheralded appearance might attract too much attention to be entirely satisfactory to the interests I was serving ... How this information was conveyed to us I may jot down some later day.... But to make a note of it is sufficient for my purpose now ... There are other wild beasts in these mountains besides panthers to account for the death of a man WHO KNOWS TOO MUCH.

"... Were it not for a positive FEELING of dread that has followed me since I threw milk into that Hindu's eyes, I should like to describe the many fascinating spots encountered in the embrace of a squalid and picturesque degeneracy.... I should linger with my brush over the opalescent lake and the sweet, calm repose of Seranagur with its purling river scouring the festooned landings and retiring abodes of tranquillity and ease,--I should like to jot down the scenes of bathers at their twilight dips when both sexes mingle as innocent as our First Parents were of a bathing costume and as devoutly fervent in their ablutions as the fabled Peris of this Paradise themselves. But there is a feeling in the air that some one is pursuing us and which cuts these memorandums short...."

46. "For purposes of self-protection I shall no longer jot down exactly our location," the next entry reads. I note merely that we are somewhere in Little Thibet and that I have met the MAN IN YELLOW ROBES AND YELLOW TURBAN AT THE LOW WHITE MONASTERY as I was told to do in the Memorandum *at Berlin.... And I approached him with the RIGHT FOOT first, my hands held in the appropriate position, until he asked me in excellent French: 'Whence come you?' Then I made the proper sign and whispered the name of the room adjacent to another room which satisfied the Lama that I was the bearer of a MESSAGE to the Exalted Dalai-Lama as well as the principal Khutuktus of the EAST.... My little audience was much mystified, BUT the MAN IN YELLOW ROBES understood.... He began whirling a brass prayer wheel as he advanced toward my 'prisoner' and salaamed.... Then laying his right hand on the 'prisoner's' shoulder the Lama said: 'Your credentials, sahib, are correct,--and it is well; as your misfortunes have been great, great will be the blessings that will fall upon thy family and thy name. Thy piety hath been known to all my brethren, likewise thy toleration,--although the INFIDEL hath been a thorn pressed evilly against thy side ...* beware of that same infidel today! He is plotting evil HERE against thy very life,--he envieth the lives of thine!... A religious war now breweth in this land!...

SPIES haunt thy footsteps from the rising to the setting sun.... BEWARE lest thy fair daughters and thy wife shall disappear!... Our prayers, sahib, shall attend thee; and our numerous eyes shall remain open to the PERILS as thou goest EAST where arms are open to receive thee,--but see thou, sahib, THAT THOU DOST WALK DILIGENTLY IN THE DIRECTION OF THOSE ARMS!...

"... The Lama backed away.... Never did he cease whirling the prayer wheel as he spoke ... this constitutes the perpetual prayer of Lamas, the theory being that the wheel communicates the petition to the air and, thus, mingled with the elements, it ascends naturally to the heaven of the blessed.... We were then conducted through a long row of very low rooms ornamented with a variety of Buddhist statues that have never been dusted nor apparently disturbed, to an open terrace which over-looked a dreary waste of gray rocks and broken ledges and offered to our view the slender roadway that lay like a ribbon across the plain until it faded into the golden glow of the Eastern horizon.... When I looked at that single road, and recalled the WARNING of the Lama so solemnly given to my 'prisoner' about the care to be given to his daughters, I REALIZED FULLY THE MEANING OF THE PRYING EYES that followed us everywhere after my encounter with the milk-fed MUSSUL-MAN disguised as a Hindu mendicant!..."

XIII
AN ENEMY IN PURSUIT

47. Local color is given in this note:

"We have had an exciting day.... The strategy one must sometimes employ in traveling through a hostile country is based upon the principle of deception.... It was the work of Maria too, who had evidently been reading up on certain occult works of the Eastern magicians and brought them into play at a moment when we were surrounded by a band of marauders in the company of my 'Hindu' friend.... To explain: There is a certain kind of little animal held sacred among these strolling outlaws.... The possession of one of these animals is supposed to be a guarantee of future happiness as well as a protection against all danger.... They are very hard to entrap and the Ladakian Islamites will spend a month endeavoring to ensnare one.... We were quite a distance from the convent at Saspoula, where the road runs around among the rocks and turns back upon itself like a horseshoe in the wooded hills.... At one of these bends the pursuers had encamped ready to dash down upon us as we turned the bend and make away with the girls in the direction of their camp in the secluded mountain passes.... Maria had secured a number of those little animals, and, twisting a fine hairpin around one of their hind legs, she let one by one escape.... The animals clambered toward the higher elevations where the banditti lay in waiting.... Their movements being impeded by the hair pins on their legs they offered an apparently easy PRIZE to the superstitious Islamites.... Abandoning their present enterprise against our party they dashed after the deceptive animals and disappeared over the hills in a mad scamper for GOOD LUCK.... This little ruse cleared our pathway and permitted us to reach Saspoula before the sun had set.... Here we passed a number of shrines besides the French and Thibetan convents.... Avoiding the convent with the tri-color floating from its mast we approached the other.... Here again were the dusty idols, banners and flags thrown into one corner, the floors littered with ugly masks and prayer wheels and books and rolls upon rolls of sacred papers mutely breathing their delegated prayers.

"... As we had been informed, the lamas here were ready to receive us, with meal and beds prepared and our own apartments all in order.... The Lama who greeted us was about five feet tall, low flat forehead, flat nose, full thick lips, rather round small head and with a sweep of black whiskers falling from his chin.... In fact, NONE of these lamas are GRAY,--the only thing that suggests AGE is their stooped and slender bodies and bent and bony fingers.... AND THEY ALLOW THE PRACTICE OF POLYANDRY in their diocese!... One woman has a dozen husbands ... and every THIRD man we meet with is a lama.

"... Still the women we see here are more attractive than those we encountered in Cashmere.

"... Before leaving the convent we were again cautioned against holding conversation with STRANGERS we might encounter in the numerous caravans along the road to LEH.... We punctiliously obeyed these instructions during the rest of our journey until we reached the PETAK convent, which stands upon an isolated rock beside an abandoned garrison or fort, with its two towers looking like ant hills beside the majestic mountain that rises ten thousand feet above our resting place.... This mountain is the sentinel that protects our entrance into Thibet.... Six miles away is LEH, elevated eleven thousand feet above the lowlands and around whose shadowy convents rise those immense granite pinnacles to an elevation of eighteen thousand feet, where their frosty crests are enshrouded in the fezzes of eternal snows!...

"... Leh, with its circlet of stubby aspen trees, its succession of terraces, its old fort and the palace of its forgotten Moguls, has its arms outstretched for us.... The mystic word has been passed along our route and BEHOLD we are encamped in a well-furnished three-story white bungalow with odors oozing from the kitchen that promise a night of security and content!..."

48. The next entry gives a glimpse of the country through which our party passed:

"Traveling toward the east we have passed through a number of villages of neat two-story houses in these narrow walled-in valleys.... The inhabitants are, clearly, of a Mongolian race,--the homeliest I have ever seen!... They cultivate but little patches of the land, sit around all day and gain their hollow cheeks and shrunken chests and wrinkled foreheads by squinting at the sun.... Even the women are tiny things with a perpetual smile that pushes up their high cheek bones into a horn-like prominence and apparently belies their apparent gaiety.... The belts of these men are perfect arsenals of curious-looking things.... With their cloth caps with ear flaps hanging down, their knee breeches and their linen shirts hung with a dozen prayer wheels, they characterize this country well....

"... If it were not apparently made compulsory by law these fellows would not wash their faces once a year.... They seem never to have changed their clothing until it is beginning to fall off their indolent frames.... They are so lazy that their hair falls off their heads.... And I have not yet seen a coat that does not carry the smear of their dirty hair.... That characterizes the MEN.... The WOMEN are altogether different.... They are perfect water rats and like to bathe many times a day.... Their gowns are red, worn like a shirt-waist over well-rounded shoulders, and tucked into green pantaloons at their waist line, over which is thrown an elaborately plaited skirt that reaches to their red embroidered shoes.... A lambskin is thrown over the back ... the hair dressed in Italian fashion ... the veil festooned with beads and coins and trinkets of all description ... an oriental pelisse touched with its fringe of gold.... That's the type of woman of these silent places we are traversing.... MARIA HAS DISCOVERED THE ORIGIN OF THE BOLSHEVIKI TENET OF FREE LOVE AND MARRIAGE.... Today she explained to her father that the idea was imported into Russia from this country together with the mercenary hordes from a region east of here.... 'These women,' she said, 'do not understand what one means by love.... They think it is too great a luxury to be tolerated among self-respecting people.... They believe NO MAN is good enough to monopolize a whole woman to himself.... That sort of MONOPOLY is contrary to the ethics of a first-class Communism everywhere and it must not be tolerated in this blessed Bolsheviki world!'... 'Tut-tut!' said her father. 'Please discontinue comments on subjects that no longer interest us.'... Manifestly my 'prisoner' is becoming bored by this unending and dreary pilgrimage along the camel route in the direction of the rising sun.... However, his gallantry to Alice is inexaustible, unflagging and unfailing. If she stubs her toe he wants to kiss the bruise.... Maria's comment has apparently aroused the hostility of certain personages in this camp.... If I were not positive that the thing could not be possible I'd swear the TALL square-shouldered lama is well known in Constantinople...."

XIV
WHERE THE PRISONERS DISAPPEARED

49. Then this entry reveals the sequence:

"We had been a number of days on the road,--our lives imperceptibly growing into a closer and more intimate companionship as the days ambled slowly away with the bleak snow-clad mountains that we left behind.... Descending down the slopes into a fertile valley, the hillsides terraced with a series of rice yards, and our paths softly shaded with the mulberry tree.... Behind us was the white-fringed mountain of the Lama, before us loomed the SACRED PINNACLE OF OMAY and off to the south spread an ancient walled city with steeples pointing heavenward surmounted by the CROSS.... Where the pagoda stood a thousand years ago now rise the hospital and the Christian missionary school.... Here the people walk on well-paved and broad sweeping streets and the tourists spend their afternoons promenading along the smooth and high and broad city wall.... As we approached this city a stream of 'rickshas came dashing in our direction commanded by the TALL slim 'lama' I had supposed we left behind!... The coolies appeared to understand their parts.... Quickly making a circle around us they pulled the women from their camels and tried to rope and bind my 'prisoner' and myself.

"Of course we were in full view of the consular flags of a dozen different nations; but that did not seem to bother the ringleader of this tatterdemalion mob.... My 'prisoner' fought like a demon.... He well remembered the lessons he received from Heath in the manly art of self-defense.... Right and left he boxed like a well-trained athlete delivering his dynamic punches well.... But finally the gang over-powered him and turned their undivided attention to me.... I was vainly attempting to reach the side of Maria and her sisters, whom the tall bully was forcing into a waiting 'ricksha manned by two barelegged men,--a dozen coolies pounced upon me, tore my clothing into fragments, furrowed my face with their infernal nails and actually attempted to bite me on the ears!...."

"I have no notion how well or hard I fought, but as I knocked one down another took his place as I fought my way to the side of the now bound and helpless girls.... Their hair was streaming down their backs, their faces flushed, their eyes filled with tears ... that sight maddened me!... I have been in many fights before, I have lain beside the dead in Flanders and among the Balkan highlands, I have seen blood flowing by me like a river,--and the thought of all these seemed to electrify my soul and fill my veins with steel.... I tore madly right and left.... I never struck such herculean blows before or since.

"I literally grabbed the tall man by the heels and whirled him round like a flail and tore into that gang of snarling hellhounds with cyclonic fury.... I literally mowed them down.... But finally a dull thud sounded in my ears.... A wave of light blinded both my eyes.... I knew nothing more until this morning when I awoke in a tent. Beside me was a loaf of bread and a canteen of cool water.... NOT ANOTHER SIGN OF A LIVING CREATURE IS IN SIGHT.... I am in a deep mountain gorge, leading to the south along a narrow roadway that has apparently witnessed the procession of unnumbered ages."

50. Then this entry:

"After tramping all day I finally emerged in the sight of a swift-flowing river on either bank of which, in the distance, appeared two walled-off cities of considerable size.... Foreign GUNBOATS were lying in the harbor in holiday attire.... As I approached the city a courier came running to meet me.... When he approached I drew back prepared to fight....

"But his friendliness disarmed me and I allowed him to draw near.... 'Li'l' ladee wantee see you quick; you cum foller me,' he said, and turned back from where he came.... I followed him with beating heart.... On the dock at the landing where the gunboat was steaming up MARIA met me with moistened eyes....

"She informed me in a low voice that the officer was ready to receive me and accept my orders.... And then she said,

"'Before you go I wish to thank you for all you have done for us.... If our paths should ever meet again I want you to know my heart will beat more quickly when I shall see you coming up the path.'... That said, she flung her slender arms around my neck, impulsively, and looked calmly in my eyes.... When, involuntarily, my arms showed signs of being prehensile, she sprang away quickly and flashed along the gangway to disappear, like a holy vision, behind that gray storm door!..."

51. The last entry reads:

"It has been a habit with me for many years to never be surprised.... When I appeared on deck to give the code to the commander of that vessel this habit was unmoored.... A tall, square-jawed man approached me with a twinkle in his clear blue eyes.... I looked at him inquiringly and a little reminiscently until I heard him speak.... 'I see the loaf of bread came in handy,' he said, extending me his bony hand.... 'I thought I left you at Ekaterinburg,' I exclaimed, recalling the moments we spent after our escape from the abandoned tunnel.... 'Oh,' he laughed, 'YOURS was not a one-man job; there are others in the world besides yourself intrusted with state secrets.... 'But what do you know about the bread, you just spoke of it?'

"'My company was following on behind,' he answered. 'When we came round the bend we saw you scrapping with that outlaw from Trebizond. You did quite well; you had all but three of them laid out in manly fashion when you got that clip on the back of the head. Then we stepped in and conducted your party to their present quarters ... thought it better for you to remain in the tent while the authorities here locked up those cutthroats for your disappearance.'

"'Have you the CODE WORD?' I asked.... He whispered it in my ear.... Then I lettered the order.... Finally he asked, 'Would you not like to meet my SISTER who has been so much interested in you?'

"His sister! I had never heard of her!... 'Of course!' I answered amiably enough for one completely stumped....

"He called a petty officer and said a few words in an undertone.... In a minute a radiant young woman with springing steps glided gracefully down the deck.... She was not, in her present attire, much different from Maria ... but as she drew near I noted the difference at a glance.... She came forward quickly and held out her hand. 'Congratulations, Mr. Fox!' she said smiling.... The Metropole!' I gasped,--'what brings YOU here?' 'Still asking questions!' she coquetted prettily. 'I merely called, of course, to inform you that the sapphire is in America!'... I thought hard for more than a minute.... Then it occurred to me that I had seen her in a dozen disguises shadowing me from Buckingham to the room upstairs on Downing Street,-

-to charm me later at The Hague--to disappear like a will-o'-the-wisp,--then to fascinate me at the Metropole.'...

"Well, the commander of the vessel tells me that it is fourteen hundred miles down stream to Woosung *and that the voyage will take seven days from there.... With his* code *word still ringing in my ears to be repeated to one man at* Berlin, to another man in England, another in Japan, and to a dignitary in Italy, the mission I have undertaken shall have been successfully discharged, so far as history *and* public policy *is concerned.... But there is* another *mission that I shall, some day, undertake that will be enshrined in lovely memories and lively fancies until* that day shall come."

PART TWO

INTRODUCTION

The daring reference by Fox, in the foregoing, to personages and events, to locations and the life incident thereto, that may easily be confuted are they false in any of their details, leads to but one conclusion.

Yet there are other incidents that reinforce that conclusion, that are only casually touched upon by Fox. The references to "the Performer at the Metropole" who "is a Baroness sure enough" and to the person named as "Syvorotka," in whom the Baroness is interested, display an unconscious connection between the mysterious underground diplomats and the Secret Agents who were acting independently in the rescue, and supplementing the activities of Fox, will be found to be fully authenticated in the vivid incidents recorded by the diarist of Part Two.

This diarist was doubtless a Russian gentleman of the official class, of elevated standing with the former Government, and of pronounced aristocratic sentiments. His previous official connections seem to have been with the High Administration, the Ministry of Finance, or with the Council of Ministers. Like many others of his class in the old regime, when the Revolution broke, he was forced to degrade himself and mingle with the evil elements that were bent on loot and rapine. By May, 1918, he appears to have been transformed into a perfect type of "Red" that deceived and terrorized the Russian population and gave credence to the Bolshevik assertion that "former officialdom is now acting with the proletariat." How well the diarist deceives the Bolsheviki and sustains this claim of Trotzky is fully revealed in the dramatic incidents recorded: nowhere in literature is found a better illustration of social metempsychosis,--of the abasement of moral and intellectual refinement to the elemental and unconscious vulgarity and irresponsibility of predatory Communism and mob indifference to shame! It is the devolution of Moral Responsibility into organized iniquity and characterizes primordial Passion released from sentiment and law,--and it was the necessary camouflage of the diarist in his struggle for life and in his efforts to promote the Czar's escape.

In translating Part Two, or the memoranda of this Imperial rescuer, from Russian into English, or the frequent French, to characterize the event recorded, there were found to be many situations, phrases and expressions that may shock the sensitive reader; in the conceptions of the diarist, however, in his cynicism and degradation he photographs Red Russia *and reveals the characteristics necessary to visualize the horror that accompanied the event. A truthful picture of this unique segment of human history can be preserved only in a* word-for-word translation of this document. Therefore, with the exception of a few letters involving the name of A.F. Kerensky, nothing has been withheld from the inspection of the reader to view the conduct of nobility subjected to privations, temptation and the fascinating power of sin.

TRANSLATOR.

I. PETROGRAD
1.

... and, post factum, everybody claims that "he (or more often she) predicted it long ago, but they would not listen." It is a lie; we all knew that the war has been conducted abominably, that Rasputin and Stuermer were plotting, that the administration was greatly inclined to graft,--all gossip of the town. But no one whom I had seen since the execution of the monk was aware of the real fact: the revolution was in the air. Rodzianko, to whom I spoke at the Club only a fortnight before the abdication, said that everything would turn out all right. In fact, the Court, and people around it,--were much better posted; perhaps they felt something growing instinctively, as they were too silly to crystallize their fears in some concrete conception. Maroossia was in Tsarskoye Selo not long before the old Admiral's death; they said that the danger was expected from the "Town and Country Union." But all these whispers and chatterings were always of the category of a "so-and-so, whose brother's friend knew a man who...."

With all my running around about the town I must confess I did not notice any movement; I always thought that the reason of the unrest--was the shortage of food, and a little provocation, to put Stuermer in a disagreeable position. The realization of the serious danger approaching all of us came to me only when the police fired on the mob on the Nevsky and the first real clash took place. I happened to cross the Liteinyi near Basseinaya Street, when I heard for the first time in my life the whistling of bullets and the peculiar drumming of the machine guns. I felt weak in the knees and around the waist and had to stand in a porte-cochere for a while. It was only for a few moments, and I felt ashamed of this disgusting feeling of fear. A crowd of cooks, or maids, passed near me shouting and screaming for help; they had disgustingly lost their self-control. I reached home in a hurry and found Maroossia pale and frightened. I had to tell her not to show her nose in the streets. Then Mikhalovsky called me up and asked how did I like the revolution. He did not like it: his cook had been shot in the knee; a very moderate cook, in fact.

2.

Committees, everywhere committees! Everywhere suspicions! No more cheerful faces! Permanent meetings of the new elements! Much conversation! Greetings! Wishes of prosperous free life! Hopes of the Allies that we will continue the war!

All this still characterizes our poor country.

Today--for the first time in my life (it is only the beginning!) I saw a real communist alive. He was a man of rather short size and dark complexion, if such could be detected under his greasy cheeks. He wore a small beard twisted at the end in a tin hook. His ears--transparent and pale--were unproportionately big. I stopped near the Elisseiev store to buy score cards for this evening's bridge, when a little group of men--civilians and soldiers--gathered near the communist. The usual crowd of nowadays loafers,--shabby looking, discussing something, casting around looks full of hostility, hatred and superiority. A boy brought a chair from a cigar counter, and the communist stepped on it, and started his talk. "Tovarishshi," he said, "the time has come."... They all applauded, though nobody knew what was going to be next, and the speaker could even have been a reactionary.

"This is he," shouted a sailor to me; a big chap with hair falling off of his cap.

"Who is he?" I questioned.

"You, burjooi," a soldier said to me, "no wonder you do not know him. This is Comrade Trotzky. He comes from America. You had better move on or I'll tell who you are,"--he continued staring at me very resolutely, and spat on the sidewalk right near my foot.

I moved on. What people!

I crossed Nevsky and stood on the other side. From there I could not hear Comrade Trotzky, but studied his movements and gesticulation, his manner of scratching his nose, of quickly turning his head in a derby, and the nervous shrugging of his shoulders. The mob applauded him after every phrase, making his speech a series of separate sentences and thus giving him the advantage of thinking of most radical ideas, while awaiting for the listeners to finish the applause.

I have finally decided to give in my resignation. What is the use? No work is being done. We only talk. The whole administration, the whole administrative machinery, stands still, evidently retrograding every day.

Many understand it. Rodzianko is going away south; a man whom they think too old and too much of a reactionary. He is quite depressed, I presume, but likes to look perfectly satisfied. When I asked him whether the war looked to him as though it were to be continued, he gazed at me, and not after hesitation sighed, and said:

"Yes, if the army will stand the effects of order number one."

And then, fearing the next question coming, he assumed the air of a busy man and shook hands--"as he had to go and see his relatives."

Nearing the house I saw Kerensky in the Emperor's car, proud, and smiling to left and right. His Excellency, the Minister of Justice!

3.

Everybody is sure and proud that he is building up the new Russia. Lawyers and doctors, engineers and priests, all run with busy faces,--they think a statesman of today must run,--everybody gives orders, counter-orders, nobody carries them out, nobody listens. There are about 200,000 Napoleons in Petrograd today; as they multiply by section, this number will be enormous before long. The situation, however, does not improve....

In the office there was quite a discussion of the probabilities, and I was listening to the younger people. Criticism and "my own opinion" are the main sicknesses. Perhaps the private initiative used to be so hardly oppressed, that it comes out at present in excess.

Why should lawyers be convinced, that their profession gives them the right, primo genio to be statesmen? I should suggest an archeologist, or a man in charge of a lighthouse.

4.

We all went to the "Farce," Maroossia and F., myself and Misha. Afterwards we had supper. At the next table to us were the M's., Alexander Ivanitsky and the Baroness B. Since her return she certainly looks much better. At first I did not see her, then before all she reprimanded me in her usual kind manner. She had grown a little thinner and has more jewelry I should say, and is as fascinating as before. When she speaks one can see that she thinks of far distant things.

"We all are busy these days," she said, when I asked her whether she came here from England just for curiosity to see all of us under the Provisional Government. "You did not change at all." Misha, who did not know B. before, did not like her very much,--in fact, they all think she is suspicious. Aren't these youngsters peculiar? Especially Misha who is so grouchy lately--all seems dangerous to him. I never think that a woman can be anything but pretty or hideous. There is no middle, and no suspicion about them. If a woman is, what they perhaps would call "suspicious"--then there is a man's influence behind her--so find the man (and it is easy) and she is as plain as a card on the table. Baroness B. is pretty. And if she likes to talk like a Pythia,--that's her way of making people interested in her.

Maroossia complained of a headache, so we left early. Baroness is in the Hotel d'Europe--she is so sorry that "her Astoria" became such a hole. Well--not only her Astoria.

5.

It certainly would be a wonder to expect anything but confusion from the men who recently became the leaders of 180 millions. The leaders are sure they can make wonders.

Prince Lvov! This old squeaking carriage, as Polenov says, is a man from whom I would not expect anything. It is enough to look at his beard, with remnants of yesterday's dinner on it, at his small blue foxy eyes always reddish and always dropping tears. Miliukov! Minister of Foreign Affairs! All his experience consists of a continuous chain of political breaks and a series of moderately paid, superficial articles on Balkan questions in a provincial newspaper. And, Monsieur Kerensky,-- la fine fleur--the Minister of Justice, a little man with a single kidney and a double ambition. Insects!

These people would not be able to administer a small country community, and here they are confronted with three immense propositions: the Great War, the building up of a new state, and the fighting of an organized propaganda directed against the war, and against order.

It was enough for the ladies (and for Maroossia too) to see all of these people in power, in order to find interesting points, not only in their political activities, that would not be so bad--but in their private lives too. They all already know who these people are, what they eat, when and where they were born, what their wives and mistresses look like, etc., etc., up to the most intimate deeds and traits of their characters. The foreign ladies also take a very keen interest in those little tea-chats. All prefer to listen to them much rather than to the events at the front.

Vadbolsky wrote me a letter sent through the "Help the Soldiers" society. Of course he could not say much. They all realize that discipline is going down with tremendous speed, at least at the Northern front. The soldiers listen more to what the Council of Deputies say than to anything else. This treble power--the Council, the Government and the Army Authorities--must be united, but there is no one to realize it; and if there were, there would be no possibility of co-ordinating the different currents.

6.

Evening with the Ivanitskys.

After dinner we all went into the library and started as usual to speak of our very bad affairs, the high cost of living, even here, in a private home, reserved, not to be accused of reactionary tastes. The ladies looked at every one who would start to talk, as if he would be the man to solve all of our complicated problems and mishaps.

Baroness B., whom I had seen very much lately, talked to me for a while in a corner, to the ridiculous anger of Maroossia who went to bed tonight without kissing me. She (the Baroness) said that Sophie had already reached London after the stay in Copenhagen and Paris. "Her mission," she said,--as usual coquettishly and childishly looking around with a fear of being overheard,--"was a failure." In Copenhagen "they would not even listen", to Sophie, and she was told that the solution and the "demarches" must be made, if made, from London, as there people have every means to arrange with Berlin. I asked the Baroness to keep all of this news to herself, and not to drag me, or what would be worse, Maroossia, into any conspiracy. "Be just as you are and don't try to become more serious, it may spoil you"--. Heavens knows what the Baroness has become since her peculiar conduct with the Vassilchikov and her permanent whisperings to Madame Vyrubov and the rest of the gang. But still, there was already a movement about Tsarskoe Selo. If I were not so particular about avoiding silly conversations, I would have asked her what she meant by communicating Sophie's failure to me.

Finally, I am glad, I did not ask her questions. What is the use of the Emperor's release to me? A man who did not know how to pick his advisors, who did not know how to arrange his home affairs, his Alice von Hessen Darmstadt, his monks and his generals, does not deserve to be too much regretted, and certainly does not deserve too particular interest. Baroness B's. actions are strange. Is she paid? By whom? Cash? Promises?...

(a page missing)

... was stopped by me and slightly pursed her red lips, we joined the rest, where a British Major (I never can think of his name) was telling of his experiences in the research work for German propaganda in Petrograd. So sorry he had to speak French with his typical Anglo-Saxon struggles with "D" and "T," that makes French so perfectly ununderstandable in an English mouth. It is horrid that people like the Ivanitskys don't know English well enough, and now, when we all have to be among our British allies, we make ourselves, and the allies as well, simply ridiculous!

So the Major explained that their man was at several meetings of a body, which he called "Le conseil secret du parti bolchevique" (that must have been something very bad indeed), where a man by name Lenine was present, also communists Bronstein, Nakhamkes, Kohan, Schwarz and others, I forget. They all are conspiring. "Be no war with our brethren," "Be peace on earth," "Closer together peasants and soldiers, workingmen and poor," "To hell with the intelligentzia," "Long live the International," etc., etc., was all we saw on the banners lately. The queerest thing is that the British agent at the meeting saw amongst the anarchists several men from the police, and a fellow by name of Petrov, the same one that had the accident on the Moscow railway and was asked to leave the Foreign Office a couple of years ago. Now Petrov is with the communists. Again the agent reported the presence of the 1905 blackhundreds. They all are there, and instead the "Boje Tsaria Khrani," they shout the International. They all understand their people (the agent said) and they all are with the Lenine and others, to return to the sweet past by destroying the bitter present. Sir George, the Major continued, knew all about these significant political blocks, and reported them to London, but the Foreign Office and the Conseil de Guerre seem to be either ignorant (I would not be very much surprised), or know more than the Ambassador, so, as yet, our Cabinet has not been warned. Our Cabinet! It sounds majestic.... Since Miliukov left, and the mercantile Monsieur Tereshchenko took his hot seat--everything goes to the devil with our policy abroad. It is strange, for Mr. Tereshchenko must be well posted in foreign relations: both of his French twin mistresses gave him every possibility of becoming "bien verse."

But--oh, shades of Count Nesselrode and Prince Gorchakov! Inspire the newcomer, looking from the walls of the Foreign Office, at his struggles! Your illegitimate son needs your sense and help ...

7.

Since the scandalous discovery of the plot (Mr. Kerensky took personal care to make it scandalous)--perhaps it was not a plot, but just a few letters of the Gr. Duchess M.P., Tsarskoye Selo has become very difficult to reach and to visit. A few days ago Maroossia came home from A. very late and so tired that I thought she was ill. The communication seems completely stopped, and soldiers were looking in the automobile every five minutes. Once she thought they would arrest her. Sentinels not only around the Palace, but in the garden too, with a double chain of Reds on the streets! The General told Maroossia that some one explained to him that these difficulties and impediments were provoked by the successes of the Germans on the Riga front, and that they expect a serious drive on Petrograd, and twice insinuated about her going to Yalta, or Gurzoof, or Gagry,--as things there rapidly were becoming complicated. So said the Admiral too, in his peculiar way: "The rats before a shipwreck usually feel the coming wreck by instinct, and run on the decks." He said that was his impression in Tsarskoye. Every rat is exceedingly nervous and tries to disappear from the Palace under some pretext or other, and the Palace is deserted.

Kerensky is coming there very often, usually with his milk-fed A.D.C.... This man wants to be generous, he wants to be square, in fact,--he wants to be magnificent. He calls the Emperor "Colonel Romanov," or "Nikolai Alexandrovich." Never says, "Your Majesty." He feels sure that he is beloved in Tsarskoye, and that they speak of him with tears of gratitude, admiring his justice and his manners. I hardly think Kerensky realizes that they are simply frightened, and feel with their inborn appreciation of the man, that by playing on his exceedingly well developed self-veneration--they might be saved. I have been told in the Club that the Government is planning to get rid somehow of the whole family. The foxy old Polenov explained to us after bridge that he would not be surprised if Kerensky would say to the Lenine crowd that the Emperor should be taken somewhere in the country on account of the German advance, and to Buchanan ... on account of the growing strength of Lenine. "Many more people are interested in this affair," he said, "than even Kerensky knows. If he knew, he would have a larger field for bargaining."

Devil knows who is who now! If police officers enlist in the communists,-- what is next? Trotzky's going to a high mass?

8.

Dined with Buchanans and the Lazarevs. Ros. was wounded. We all enjoyed this little story:--

A German girl was asked:

"Koennen sie Ibsen?" To which she replied:

"Nein! Wie macht man das?"

9.

I suspected, and feared, that it could or might have happened,--and so it was!

Yesterday Mikhalovsky asked me to come to his office. He looked queer and worried, and when I stepped in, he closed the door and started to reproach me with every sign of excitement, so proper to him; spitting all over my face.

"I never expected that from you! I never expected! How is it? What is it!?..." and so on.

I stopped him and asked him to be more explicit, as I could not grasp all of the meaning of his eloquence. After he lit a cigarette (how many times this little thing has been a salvation!) Mikhalovsky became more comprehensible and told me that Misha phoned at one o'clock in the night and asked him to come immediately to the Intelligence in his private office. Mikhalovsky, who is now taking great care of himself, drinks some waters, takes green pills and goes to bed at nine, became enraged and refused, but Misha said he was an ass, and simply had to dress and go to the headquarters. So the old thing had to dress and appear. Misha showed him a short note from the French Agent which read something like this:--"Baroness B. evidently communicating with Copenhagen through Sharp and Starleit M. General Z. to be approached, also Quart.--General R. In one instance a package carried to Sestroretsk by a lady in a blue tailor suit with white fox fur. Trail lady, arrest Baroness B. Watch Finland Depot, radio to Generals Z. and R." No signature.

My astonishment was very great, and I said that "though I have known Baroness B. quite well since I met her in Paris and Monte Carlo and...."

(five lines scratched out from manuscript).... "Quit your damn jokes for a while," he exclaimed. "Do you realize, what you are talking about? The lady with the fox--is Maroossia!"

"Maroossia? Spying?" I said, becoming angry in my turn. "You will have to account for it, Boris Platonovich, as even an old friend and relative must think over those accusations."

Then Mikhalovsky explained that Misha's man followed the lady--up to the house, and that it was Maroossia. Another one "listened in," and understood from

Maroossia's and Baroness B's. conversation, that my wife took the package to a certain Madame van der Huechts in Sestroretsk, on being told to do so by the Baroness, and that she did not know what there was in it, and even did not know who Madame van der Huechts was.

"You see, you boneheaded fool," Mikhalovsky continued, "what was the danger? If Misha had not succeeded in having his own man listen in, and do it quietly, all of this detective work, your Maroossia would be gone by this time." "But,"--he continued, "now the case is closed, as far as your wife is concerned, and the only thing I wish to insist upon,--is to get Maroossia out of here right now. Furthermore, you should give her a scolding."

I said it would not be omitted.

10.

Maroossia left for her father's. We certainly had some explanation! She cried and felt indignant, and finally understood why I was so angry when the evening papers came out with the news of Baroness B's arrest. Then--she understood that she never should do anything that was asked her "without her husband's knowledge." The case, as Mikhalovsky says, is closed.

The last two or three evenings I spent with both Mikhalovskys. They told me strange stories. I simply cannot believe them. First--that the German staff sent Lenine here with a special message to some people now in power. "We know all about it," said Misha, "but the time is not yet ripe to act." Second--that a certain person received a request not to touch Grimm, nor any of the communists. Third--the strangest--to get the Tsar's family out. "All of this news would have been much fuller if only we could decipher some of this,"--and Misha took out of his pocket and presented me with this strange slip of paper....

(missing)

...--all of these crossings of the lines are words, or ciphers, or phrases, God knows what, and they must mean something very important for they were taken from members of this web, and stand in direct connection with our present, or rather our future, attitude. But that is about as much as we know of it.

11.

I went to Cubat's for luncheon, as the cook had to go to a meeting,--how do you like that?--and I do not regret it, for I learned much.

When I think of Cubat's, Contant's or the Hotel de France's public before the war, and compare them with the present, I find the difference on the style of people simply enormous. They never were here before,--these types of men with eyes looking for quick money, for instantaneous riches, for some "affaires du ravitaillement militaire." Yesterday's poor chaps, that would not know the difference between a cotelette and a jigot are ordering and easily eating things that it would take me some time to think of. Democratisation of French cooking, or vulgarisation of exclusive tastes (?) which?

I met Frank at Cubat's.... Heaven knows how he got released from custody. I could not help it when he approached my table and greeted me; I asked him whether he had heard anything from Colonel Makevich. He asked me about Maroossia, so one thing led to another, and finally the waiter brought a chair. "Can I join you?" he asked. I growled something like "delighted" and so he sat down. The conversation at first was rather general, and then suddenly:

"Did you hear anything of the Baroness B's. case, and how is she now?" he said.

This unexpected question put Frank in a new light. I had to take several puffs of my cigarette to think over my answer. Frank gave me time to prepare the response in giving orders to the maitre d'hotel. Quite a bit of time elapsed after he questioned me. I hoped for an instant that he was going to forget about it, but, alas, when he was through with his orders (from which I understood that he either had become rich, or expected me to pay his check) he looked at me and repeated:

"Yes, sir, did you hear anything new of the poor Baroness?"

"Well," I replied, "the only thing that we all know: she is in jail."

"Your information," he smiled, "is quite old. They released her about a day or two after this misunderstanding was cleared up."

"What do you mean 'misunderstanding.' You would not call such a case so gently, I suppose?"

"Here we are!" Frank said, lowering his voice. "So you must know more than the average person. I, personally, knew only that there was an arrest, and a release (as I saw the Baroness) after they understood that there was no reason for holding a perfectly loyal lady. I think we should talk it over again, but not here. I read in the Town Activities column that your wife went to Tula. Couldn't you join me for dinner tonight at Contant, say at seven-thirty?"

My first impulse was to refuse him flat. Then I happened to think that my avoiding him would perhaps somehow reflect on Maroossia for her silly behavior with the package. Besides I was interested to know what Frank would talk about, and to know what happened to the B. And again it interested me to know what he was doing at present. So I hesitated.

"Please do, decide affirmatively," he begged. "I feel sure you will not regret a good dinner."

"Very well," I said, "at seven-thirty."

After luncheon I crossed the street to see Mikhalovsky, whom I was sure to find in the Club. He was going out with Polenov.

"Aha, dear boy!" Polenov said to me. "The wife is away, and here he runs around like--... (his comparisons are striking, but very rough!) Come on with me. There are no political parties or platforms at Nadejda Stepanovna. A little lawyer, and an old soldier are equally welcome. Nadejda Stepanovna just telephoned there are new ones."

The old fool! As if there was a single living being in the town that would not know that all his pleasures were reduced to kissing a new girl on the forehead and petting her behind the ears! Nadejda Stepanovna told me how they all laughed watching Polenov through the keyhole.... "Thanks," I said, "I am through with the Oficerskaya Street." So he went alone, trying to look younger and straighter.

When he left I asked Makhalovsky to explain to me what happened to the Baroness. He almost fainted.

"For heavens sake! Don't shout that damned name! There are ears everywhere," he whispered.

He took me by the arm and dragged me all along the Morskaya, giving me short and hard kicks as soon as I would open my mouth. And only when we reached his room and he verified as to whether or not the door was well shut, he said:

"Now what seems to be your question, and what in hell do you know about her? Who told you that something happened to her?"

As this is the time when "homo homini--lupus," I said that nobody ever told me of her, but having met Mikhalovsky at the Club I thought of the Baroness and asked.

"Well," he said, "she was released." And Mikhalovsky became sad and worried, looking humble and frightened.

"I am all tangled up, friend!" he said. "I think I am in mortal danger. Last Friday Kerensky asked me to come to his office and said she must be freed, and everything was a misunderstanding. He said he had received proof; her arrest was a mistake. He also said that we all must be careful about our arrests, "from the left, as well as from the right."

"Did the British Embassy intervene?"--"Not at all (it seems though they never had heared of it)."

--"and here," he continued, "we received a letter signed by Executive Committee, Department of Political Research, saying that unless the whole dossier of the Baroness B. was burned, the undersigned of the message reserved the privilege of knowing how to deal with it. Misha was so disgusted with the letter that he went to see Kerensky, and explained that a body of doubtful prerogatives and no official standing had no right to insult an official institution by threats. Kerensky read the letter, studied the attached signatures and said "that he would not pay any particular attention to the letter, that there was decidedly no reason to think that the authority of the Department was offended, or held in contempt." He took the letter from Misha saying that "as I see it affects you too much, I will make a private and personal investigation and let you know when I get some results."

"Now," Mikhalovsky continued, lowering his voice, "Misha has disappeared. He is not in the office. He has never come home since the morning he told me all of that. When I asked his chief whether he knew anything about Misha--I got an answer that he was looking for him all over the city and could find neither Misha nor a dossier which he needs more than Misha himself! I feel,--I know, Misha is dead. And surely, all that in connection...."

"Look here, Boris Platonovich," I said, "You must not feel so terribly depressed about that story. Nothing happened to Misha ..." and I continued in that tone of consolation, though I knew how weak the words sounded.

Mikhalovsky shook his head. "Anyhow I won't let it pass so easily. I'll try to know, and I'll try to clear it out...."

I left him with his head down on his hands, in an agony of sorrow for Misha, and in an agony of fears for his own sake.

At about twenty to eight I entered the restaurant, having decided to keep silent, to give no chance to the man to understand me not only by questions, but even by the association of ideas: I decided to be like stone. He was talking to a chap in the hall, a tall, pimply young man of twenty-five, in the French style of blue khaki and with aviation insignia on his sleeve. Frank left his friend and we both went to the dining room.

When we were through with our soup, Frank said:

"I have touched today upon the case of the Baroness. In fact you know the story from many sources, especially from Mikholavsky.... Please, please!" he exclaimed, when I made a movement of protest,--"don't. So, if you are apt in making logical decisions and conclusions, you are in a position to understand all. Don't try to destroy anything by going around with your personal impressions, for it really would be bad. Just look!"

The telegram he showed me read: "Michael Mikhalovsky's body found on the track near Vyborg station four in the morning suicide presumed." "There is no need for explanations," he said, in putting the message back in his pocket, "nor sorrow--all is over. But it would be an excellent idea to appreciate this mere fact properly, don't you think so?"

"So," continued Frank, "to come closer to our own affairs, I must say that a young and charming lady is leaving for Stockholm on a special mission--I know not exactly what it is--and I must give her some information, some of which could be furnished by you. Before I ask you for this little information, however, I must clearly apprehend one thing: do you feel sufficiently interested in anything closely connected with the old regime? And if so,--how deep is your interest? You understand?"

"I understand," I said, after a second of thinking. "I also get your threat. Now--my answer will be clearer than your insinuations, as I fear nothing that I cannot see." (what a liar I am!)

Then I assumed my best poker face and calmly continued:

"I don't know, and do not care to know, what you are after, Frank. Personally--I cannot find anything in the old regime that I would regret to any important extent. On the other hand--I honestly do not see anything attractive, or particularly elegant, about the new regime. Practically there is no regime whatsoever in this present concoction of kuvaka and elevated ideas. So, finally, damn it all! I would be grateful to a friend who would advise me how to get out of any activity, and of course, would not consider any suggestion leading me into it. My decision is plain. I resign. Then I realize all I can and disappear from this rich field of political life. That's all, Frank."

He looked at me. He was very grave. And then suddenly his face changed and he again became the chap that amused Maroossia and myself in Marienbad a few years ago.

"So I feel, old man, exactly so," he laughed,--"aren't all of them the rottenest types one ever saw? Trash, my dear sir, trash. And I greet your decision."

The tension which I felt at the beginning of the dinner disappeared completely, and we began to talk about different things, remembering the time when we met, and recollecting our mutual impressions of 1912-1913, when things and people seemed to be so very different. I could not help, however, asking Frank at the end of our dinner:

"Are there any especial reasons to try and be foxy with me, or any reasons to frighten me with mysteries?"

He answered:...

(several lines scratched out)

..."no such things as mysteries. This is the commonest of all planets and everything is plain and entirely within the old three dimensions. Some very cautious persons do not see the matter clearly--or perhaps they are too stubborn to see it right,--and it makes them suspicious.... You'll kindly forgive me," he added, "if I'll have to be going?"...

After his departure--it was only about 9:30, as I had nothing to do, I went to the New Club. No Misha there. I saw Boris Vlad. drunk as a sailor in company with three or four other rascals; I think the short one was the man from the Red Cross. In the card room--a gloomy game of bridge, no word said unless for a real mistake....

So I came home and looked out of the window onto the deserted and neglected streets of my Northern Palmira....

12.

Millions of those who fell for their countries in Europe and Asia paved the way for a general depreciation of life; human existence has no more value. For years they were killing people on the battle fields. It is justified.... They were killing lately, in Russia, officers (for the reason that they were such.) It can be understood: the crazy mob is not responsible. But what can one think of murders? For reasons unknown to the murdered, and perhaps to the murderers. Here are the results of three years of war, the results of three hundred years of slavery.

Maroossia read the news of Mikhalovsky's accident in the papers in Tula, and came yesterday.

"Nothing could stop me," she said, crying bitterly, and leaning on me so that I would not be too angry. "Dearest, everything is so strange! Misha's death, and Boris Platonovich's death!... Please, let us go away somewhere, I cannot think of you, here alone...."

I told her that I had made arrangements to resign, and why it could not be done yet. "Then," I said, "we will go to Gurzoof, where our house is rotting without care". I succeeded in calming the poor girl, explaining with all of the eloquence that I had, that Misha's suicide and Mikhalovsky's accident in the lift had nothing in common, and that both deaths were not to be put in the same angle of view.

Later she showed me a postal card from Misha, from Vyborg. He did not sign it, but his characteristic handwriting spoke only too clearly. "Wanted to send you some fruit," he wrote, "but here there is no fruit, so you'll have to get some yourself from the South."

"Poor Misha, there was something strange about him before he killed himself," she said. "I never asked him for any fruit. He was very nervous, the poor boy, I see it! And to think that almost in his last hour he thought of us!..."

Fruit from the south.... I see Misha's dead hand pointing to us the way out of

Petrograd. It is a warning, a cipher warning from the other side of the grave; one more inducement to leave this filthy place.

13.

I again hear that something is growing amongst the bolsheviki. There are indications that if everything passes well for them--Kerensky will join the movement, passing from the left social revolutionary party to the commune. Both parties deal with internationalism, and finally the only difference is that the bolsheviki act more energetically.

The country will then become an ideal state: people would not know any laws, would not pay taxes, would not marry, or sell or buy.... Fine! About the last, however, I have my doubts. There will be always somebody to be bought in Petrograd. It is in the climate, I guess.

The Allies! Our Allies who were ready to fight Germany to the last Russian soldier.... Do they understand that the fraternization at the present time is so intense, that pretty soon the boches will get the foodstuffs from the very hands of their Russian comrades? They must know that at present there are only few men to be hanged. The war will be won in a month. Tomorrow their number will be so big, that not enough hangmen could be found in the world to clean up Russia,--unless some Powers wish to see Russia amputated. This looks probable.

Today saw the British Major. He expressed his condolence for our grief. I received the impression (or perhaps I am getting too nervous and suspicious?) that he knows more than I.

14.

Quite unexpectedly the Baroness B. came today to the office. At first I did not want to see her, but then thought that it would be better not to make these dangerous people angry, as heaven knows what they are liable to do if irritated, and besides--she is so fascinating. So she was shown in. She was veiled as much as only she could be, for mystery and to conceal the slight and ingenious coat of rouge, I guess. The usual feathers, rings and perfumes; and I had thought that I would see an ascetic face tired out by seclusion! She said that she had nothing serious to tell me, but had just run in to say good-bye and calm me; she was not going to call on Maroossia: "too busy and other reasons."

"I appreciate your other reasons," I said. "You have already shown what a friend you are. Why did you drag Maroossia into your business? You probably are well protected against any disagreeable event, but we are not. So next time please, use your other reasons...."

"There was no dragging your wife into my business. The package of laces she took to Madame van der Huechts is not a crime. Besides everything is over; so, as if nothing had happened."

"Yes, it probably is nothing. Misha would be of a different opinion, I am sure."

"No, he would not."

There was a silence for a while, and then she said, sighing: (line illegible...) "For instance, we wanted to give you the whole outline inviting you to do something for your country--and you refused to help."

"Baroness," I said, "honestly and truly I don't understand these speculations. Just as honestly and just as truly I don't care for them, no matter what they are for. I hate this manner of operation. The manner! I hate plots. I hate underground work, and the only thing I care for--is my own comfort and my own affairs."

"You don't know what you are talking about," she said, "or the atmosphere has made you so clever, that I don't know whether you are trying to get something out of me or not. Very well, I am conspiring. I am now with these people, with whom I would not have thought of being--only three months ago. As soon as I succeed--I shall leave all and become free and independent...."

Then she corrected herself; "I don't mean to say, of course, I am not independent now, but.... What time is it?"

I told her.

"Thank you. So you see.... What were we talking about?... Ah, yes, indeed,--how silly of me! Well so I am in a big game. It may seem that I am in the wrong. But think of the time when there will be a moment, when just a few persons, maybe only one person, will be able to appear again on the stage and become the nucleus of regeneration? And if I am wrong--and such moment will never come--it is so easy to get rid of those whom many persons are trying to preserve...."

"Yes," I said, smiling at her enthusiasm and innocent cynicism.

"Please omit your insinuations and sarcasm, you bad thing. I only see you are not patriotic, or you have something personal against me."

"You can judge better than others on this last point. It looks to me as though you were wrong about the rest, however...."

(a page torn out)

"... I saw Tatiana (don't ask me questions, if you please!) and the girl said that there are only two acceptable ways: to be released by the will of the people, or taken against their will, a kidnapping staged. Other methods will meet with a refusal. That is why the Emperor refused a formal foreign intervention, for it would place them in a position of parasites with the "ex" title. After everything is through--all of your Kerenskys--a parasite could not be popular and desirable.... Well, she got up,--"goodby! Kiss Maroossia for me. And here is a friendly warning: don't talk. It is dangerous. ***Don't trust.*** It is silly. Write to Sophie's house in Paris--it will reach me. So sorry we cannot be together!"

She left me.

15.

Saw a real picture of the time: General S-sky in the Renault with Joffe! Smiles and hand-shakes. Red arm-bands. The tall Dolivo-Dobrovolsky from the Foreign Office was with this couple. In January, when S-sky got his car he said: "I'd rather sell the car than let a Jew ride in it," when Gunzburg asked to use the automobile.

Madame D's apartment was robbed. Nobody knows "how it happened." The house guard keeps silent on the subject. Paul sent her a wire to Kursk, very laconic: "home emptied everything stolen." Now he received a reply: "Sublet unfurnished." She is a darling. Never saw such energy. I wonder whether she is trying to get the Emperor out too?...

16.

My interview with his Excellency is worthy of description. Since my graduation from the Lyceum up to the present time--I have seen many men of power; when young--they usually knocked me down by their aureole of magnificence; with age I learned how to distinguish almost unmistakably in the splendor of that scenery an idiot from a crook. This one--was quite peculiar.

Kerensky made me wait for about one hour during which I had enough time to ascertain that since the new regime the rooms had not been dusted. So what Kerensky said to some foreigner: "Regenerated Russia will not have recourse to the shameful methods utilized by the old regime"--were untruthful words. The dust evidently was old regime's.

At the end of the hour (it was enough for Kerensky!) I decided to go home and mail the resignation. When I got up, however, one of his men (the young rascal was watching me, I am sure) entered and asked me to step in. The staging of the reception was prearranged and intended to impress the visitor; on the desk of the Minister I saw maps and charts, specimens of tobacco for the soldiers, designs of the new scenery for the Mariinsky Theatre, models of American shells, foreign newspapers, barbed wire scissors, etc., etc., just to show the newcomer the immense range of His Excellency's occupations and duties. When I stepped in, Kerensky looked at me, posing as being exceedingly fatigued in caring for the benefit of others. He almost suffered! He never looked to me so exotic as at this moment: the Palace--and, at the same time the perspiring forehead, the dirty military outfit. The magnificence of power,--and the yellowish collar, badly shined boots. He was glad of the impression produced on me, as I registered disgust,--he, with his usual knowledge of men, thought it worship. "Look how we, new Russians, are working"--shouted his whole appearance, "look, you pig, and compare with what you have been doing!"

"Alexander Fedorovich," I said approaching him, "I thought I had to bring my resignation personally. You'll find the reasons as "family circumstances,"--and I gave him the paper.

He rose. With one hand on the buttons of his uniform and the other on the desk; he believed himself to look like Napoleon. Like Napoleon he looked straight into my eyes. But his weak and thin fingers were always moving like a small octopus--Napoleon's were stronger.

"May I ask you the real cause of your resignation?" he said, vainly forcing his high-pitched voice lower.

"If you care to know it," I said calmly,--"It is disgust."

Napoleon faded away from his face, and before me was again Monsieur Kerensky, a little lawyer with whom I had once made a trip from Moscow to Petrograd. A little lawyer who tried to please me and looked for my sympathy.

"That's the appreciation of our work!... Poor Russia! She is deserted! Here I am all alone to carry this burden"--and Kerensky showed with a circular movement of disorder on his desk,--"But you," he continued, after a pause,--"you! Why should you *be disgusted, and why should* you leave us at this strenuous moment? Don't you see that the building up of the state needs the full co-operation of every element of Russia,--the new ones, as well as the old?"

I said that I did not think I was more of an old element than he, but repeated my categoric decision.

As if wounded right in the heart, with a theatrical sigh, Kerensky looked out of the window, then smiled bitterly, and took the paper from me. "I grant you your request. I know what disgusted you,--and, and--I understand. I hope you will not regret this step."

He sat down thus politely indicating the end of the audience. Here, on his desk, I noticed one of the last numbers of the "L'Illustration" with a large picture of himself on it, which he was studying while I was waiting for his interview.

How easy I feel! Left to my own affairs, to my own business, all to my very own self! Thank God! I never felt this way before.

And our national Tartarin of Tarrascon--at his desk in the palace, with his people, always meeting polite and covetous eyes,--will continue his hard work. Under every smile and every bow, he will see--up to the grave, the veiled appreciation: "By God, what a small thing you are." On the pages of history his name will forever remain and look like the trace of a malicious and sick fly.

17.

How glad I am that Maroossia went away! I feel more at ease though the house-keeping is up to me.

There was more shooting and more of revolution, than heretofore, during all of these days,--one more evidence that the building of the new state is in full progress. Of course,--these days brought Kerensky as high up as he only can go. Next will be his precipitated downfall,--much speedier than his elevation. Why do the Allies make this mistake of letting a worm like Kerensky endanger the cause--it is a mystery ... though "there are no mysteries in this plainest of planets."

Nahkamkes and Trotzky--found! and in jail, for the moment being,--perhaps like the Baroness, or even easier! But the man, the real German hound of Petrograd, Monsieur Ulianov-Lenin,--could not be found. Could not be found is true. He has not been looked for, as any ass knows where he is. They send him meals from Felicien, or Ernest.

Away from here! I must be going as soon as I get the things straightened.

Have wired to Maroossia that I am still alive, otherwise she is liable to appear again. Elisabeth wrote a letter from Moscow and said that "here--everybody is well and things look satisfactory. Food supplies in abundance. All active in building up the state." Is she sick? Who is building the state? We destroy.

They speak of putting the Emperor in jail,--the St. Peter and Paul Fortress. On the other hand Polenov was told that Kerensky won't tolerate any abuse to "private citizens." How about other private citizens?

18.

So finally they all lost.

The Emperor was taken away,--and both Mikhalovskys died for nothing, just looking for the plotters, I think, or, perhaps, they were plotting themselves?

Mr. Kerensky did not dare to do it himself personally, as he used to say it repeatedly in Tsarskoye. No! Lies usually led him to other things: to give to the Family a "detachment of special destination" under Col. Kobylinsky (a fine man,--Emperor's A.D.C. during the Empire, and his jailer during the Republic!) and Monsieur Makarov, under whose command they all left for Tobolsk. I had to buy a map. Sorry to ascertain it, but I have always mixed up Tomsk, Tobolsk and Yakutsk. Which was which was a puzzle to me. We Russians must be proud of our perfect ignorance of Siberia.

Monsieur Makarov? Nobody knew him, but, of course, Polenov. "Oh," he said, when I told him the news, "Makarov. A man who looks like Turguenev, smells of French perfumes, speaks of the arts and is a contractor!?... Of course I know of him. He is from the "Brussov and Makarov Contracting Company"--the rascal! Kerensky knew him long ago, I am sure. The first thing when he got powerful he appointed Makarov as something in the Ministry of Beaux-Arts!"

From what I learned afterwards from Admiral and B-tov, all of "the rats of Tsarskoye" ran away. Only a few remained with the family: Botkin,--Capt. Melnik, Countess G. and her governess, M-e Sch., and Gillard. That's about all I guess that I know of--maybe some will join them afterwards. I am so sorry I had to go to Tula when they took the Family. I'd have gone to watch the departure with the Admiral.

Petrograd simply died. The city does not reflect a thing. All seem to be satisfied with mere existence, and to have lost interest in the rest of the world. They look animated when it comes time to converse of food and clothes.... Funny, strange, weird city! They don't clean the streets any more.... and everybody finds it natural. There is nothing in the stores--and we feel perfectly at ease. The country is being maliciously run down--and all repeat that fiction of building up.

Perhaps the only place that has not changed since its foundation is the Club. The same old grouches are there, on the same sized seats, with the same expressions of old indigestion and fresh gossip. Boys keep up! The revolution will probably bring the sacred card games onto the streets. Your progressive institution must preserve the classic rules for the next generations.

People now are divided into two distinct camps: those of today, and those of yesterday. The former--cover their disgust under a smile of opportunism; kin and kind--don't. We hate each other, and envy each other,--as we cannot see which way things will turn.... We will be united only if the ones of to-morrow,--the commune, the third class of people happen to take into their hands the war machinery. Then we both will be crushed, annihilated, forgotten. It is coming....

II. TUMEN

19

Only five months ago--I had a wife, income, good food.... Only five months ago--I had a country.

The mean and envious beast that lived in our midst,--as it lives in every other country,--unseen, but felt, and always ready to crush the acquirements of existing civilization,-- the mob *came out from the underground world; criminal hands let* the mob on the streets. Weak and shaky fingers unlocked the trap; a magnificent gesture of an ignorant Don Quixote invited the spies, the thieves, the murderers "to make the New Russia."

I see foreign faces around me; I hear foreign accents in every line of each new edict; I listen to the strange names of our new governors.

The Mob is in power; and the friendly faces of our Allies became dry and cold....

Looking backward--I try to find out whether there was a mistake of my own, or my own crime, for which some unknown and heartless Judge is now so severely punishing me?

*   *   *   *   *

Here I am, a graduate of the two best institutions in Russia and Germany, a man with five generations behind me,--all thoroughbred, all civilized, all gentlemen. Here I am in disguise--as apparently thousands and thousands of other Russians are, just as bearded as they, just as dirty, just as hungry, just as alone in the world.

My name is now Alexei Petrovich Syvorotka, formerly non-commissioned officer, 7th of Hussars, born in the province of Kursk. I dress in an old military overcoat, have a badly broken shoulder blade (second degree injury at Stanislau), and as my documents say--have been evacuated to Tumen, where I am supposed to receive my soldier's ration. Syvorotka! Would you talk to a man with such a name?

This Syvorotka, a humble creature--a shadow of yesterday--has only one thing of which he cannot be robbed, his only consolation: the sorrow which he wears deep under his uniform jealously concealed from the rest of the world.

20

My baggage--the handbag--was found.

Those peculiar things can happen only in the present Russia. She is like a good make of automobile after a wreck. Everything seems to be crushed and broken--machinery, wheels, glass, body.... Still some parts are strong enough to keep moving. So miraculously there moved a part, which brought my handbag here from Moscow,--the very first ray of sun in my existence for a long time.

I came to the depot this morning--I had been coming every day since Schmelin gave me the baggage check--and saw a few men unloading a baggage coach. I approached them.

"Hello," I said to a tartar whose abominable face was covered with pock marks, (nowadays one must always address the most hostile looking person in a crowd, never the most sympathetic, for one should not show any weakness to the mob), "any work"?

"Hello,--yourself," the tartar answered grouchily and without looking at me, "there is. Don't let them skin you. Ask fifty rubles, understand?"

"Is that so?" I said, spitting through my front teeth onto a sidewalk covered with gleaming white snow, "not me, damn them! Whose baggage?"

They did not answer--in their language it meant 'don't know, don't care, and go to hell!'

On the coach I saw "Moscow Special" written with white stone and I decided to take one more chance and ask for my handbag, presenting my luggage check.

"It came at last," said the man in charge of the luggage depot, "thank God I won't see your muzzle any more. What's in it?"

"Since when has it been your business, your burjooi honor?" I said, "You did not pay me for buying my belongings, so better keep your trap shut!"

I took the dear old bag--it was Maroosia's before, and came home. What did Mlle. Goroshkin put in the bag in Moscow? I opened the rusty lock--and found my silver toilet kit, razors, "La Question du Maroc," on which the shaving soap had made a big yellow spot, Laferme cigarettes, some linen (the thing I need the most), night slippers, manicuring box, and poor Maroossia's fan,--she wired me to take it to Gurzoof in the last telegram I ever got from her.

The fan was fragrant with her perfume on it; so I shed a few tears. On the inside of the bag was written "All well, write often," and on the bottom of the bag--was this book of my notes. I had decided to sell the silver kit and the fan and get some money as I was very short of it. Both the fan and the silver outfit looked so inharmonious in my little room with a small window on a triste court with a yard full of blindingly white snow.

21

Here is what brought me here:

I could not leave Petrograd on time on account of the house. Nobody wanted it for 800,000. I waited and waited--day after day, week after week. Many and many were giving me advice to leave and were warning me, but I would not listen. When the wire came that poor Maroossia was killed,--I lost interest in life completely. So I was living in Petrograd, until the clash for the Assembly. Then,--perhaps my nerves needed a good shaking up,--I became active again. I went to the Volga Kama for my money,--the were already closed and gave me 150 rubles, and allowed me to take another 150 in a week. I went to the Volkov's. The clerk said that I had no right to withdraw more than 150. I knew the man from Moscow well, and he recognized me from the time that I was coming to Bros. Djamgarov Bank. He was really kind, and said that he could at once arrange that I should receive 80% of my money and the contents in the safe, out of which 10% should be paid to some mysterious commissary. "I advise you to take it. The appetites are growing, and perhaps to-morrow it will be more,--50% or 60%." I wrote out some kind of understanding, by which I sold my rights on the 10th of October to a certain Kagajitsky. That was all fake, as my arrangement was made about the 23rd of November, I guess.

My ticket, for which they asked me 12,000 rubles, was obtained through the cook's sweetheart, and I left Petrograd on the 6th for Moscow on the usual 12:30, and arrived uneventfully at the depot in Moscow next morning at about 10:30.

On the stairs of the Nikolaevsky depot I stopped. Where was I going? In fact I had never thought of it. I had no place, no destination, no desires--nothing. Perhaps only one desire, to avenge myself and all of us.

So I hesitated, for in Moscow they had been shooting right and left for the past week, persecuting the burjois and officers. I had never felt so helpless and so unnecessary to myself and to others as on this snowy morning in Moscow. Besides, all of the way from Petrograd to Moscow I had had a hideous headache and chills, and I was in a fog of indifference.

"Good morning, sir," said an astonishingly polite voice behind me, "I congratulate you upon a safe arrival."

I turned around and saw a man of rather short stature, cleanly shaven, and politely smiling with the whole width of his mouth.

"Good morning," I said, "I cannot place you, but you seem familiar to me, I am sure."

"That's due to my former occupation, your Excellency. I am Goroshkin, the usher from the Ekaterinensky Theatre. So sorry to apprehend of your sorrow, Sir, in connection with her Excellency's death."

This man, Goroshkin, was a real friend to me, although I hardly recollected him. We never used to pay much attention to the ushers!

There was no use in trying to go to a hotel with my appearance of a gentleman and my pockets filled with money; my fever and my indifference were growing; I had no desire to do anything for myself. I think that Goroshkin understood me and the state of my mind when he said, "May I venture to offer Your Excellency my humble house, and perhaps call a doctor?"

This is as much as I remember of the next fortnight. I had a terrible attack of typhus,--and when communists were killing the boys from the military school, bombarding the Hotel National, destroying the Kremlin and pillaging private homes, I was quietly lying in a little house somewhere behind Sukharev Tower under the care of a doctor and Goroshkin's fat sister, whose conspicuous parts of the corsage were soiled from cooking, and whose face was always red and radiant. My return to life, and with it my return to the desire for activity and eating, was commemorated by the appearance at my bed of nobody else but Marchenko.

One bright morning, when my room seemed to be full of sunshine and hope,--a man in the uniform of a communist soldier with a red rag on his coat sleeve, walked into the room bringing in a breath of fresh and frosty air and a whole arsenal of munitions. I did not recognize him at first, a little pointed beard and heavy boots had transformed him into a regular "tovarishch."

"Hello," he said, "glad to know you're alive."

"Yes," I answered, "I am about the only one whom they have not happened to exterminate, but it is coming"!

Marchenko smiled. "You should not stay here for very long," he said, "It is getting dangerous and raids are being planned to finish with the burjoois who are hiding in the outskirts of Moscow."

"Don't think," he went on, "that I am honestly with the communists. My task is the same and if we failed to do something before,--now we know we will be successful. Kerensky is out of the life, living evidently under the friendly protection of Lenine; I think Lenine was the only man that he did not attempt to double cross."

"Now," he continued, "let us speak of you. I think that you must understand that the little services that were asked of you some months ago would have prevented many, many disagreeable events. Behind you, you can see only sad memories and mourning,--before you, the very dark existence of a man in hiding. If you will join us, I could guarantee you a more or less protected life,--of course you will have to care for your own self, too."

"Please your Excellency," said the voice of Goroshkin behind me, "don't refuse this time. If your esteemed father could have known the circumstances, he would have consented, and he was a strict man. I recollect that His Excellency would not deign to wait a second for his overcoat."

"Very well, I accept," I said to Marchenko, "but I must say to you that it is not for the protection you promise me. I do not care much for my life, but I would like to preserve it. Not to die right now, but hold it until the moment when I could avenge myself. And that's my personal aim. As for your plan--it suits me--for it is a measure not of Russia's good--but a weapon against our present enemy--the Red Flag. And, I may add that in me you will find a disciplined man."

Goroshkin disappeared and came back with a bottle of Abrau-Durcot, with which we celebrated my consent.

Indeed I had nothing further to think about. My task was to go to Tumen in disguise, meet some people there, and through Goroshkin communicate with Marchenko.

My instructions included....

(a few pages torn out)

22

Goroshkin brought me a passport of Mr. Syvorotka, with my description and my particular marks (broken shoulder), documents and uniform, and gave me a few names in Tumen which I had to remember and to whom on behalf of Mr. Andrei Andreivich Vysotsky I should address myself.

"Your Excellency understands that nobody assumes any responsibility for your safety. You just must be in touch with the people," he said, "and be ready for what you were told to do, as we must have a man in Tumen. If I may suggest, you should not speak or act like a gentleman."

I decided to joke a bit with Goroshkin: "Go to hell, you old fool," I said, "you damned plotter," and then I kicked a chair.

To my great astonishment not a muscle twitched in Goroshkin's face.

"Not bad, not bad," he said calmly, "but even your slang is a gentleman's. Your Excellency should imagine having been born a swine. That's the point. I should recommend more of silence, and if you happen to speak,--a brief articulation, roughly conceived and expressed. Don't bother at all with the person you are addressing."

The old man amused me very much that evening. I let him sit down and he told me episodes of his life for about a couple of hours. For thirty years he had been present at every performance in his theatre and he knew the world better than I did, only by watching the artists.

January the tenth in the early morning at about six o'clock the fat Mlle. Goroshkin entered my room clad only in a nightgown. That was the only time I saw her pale and sordid, but she was just as uninteresting as ever. "Quick! Get up," she said, "they are searching. Brother has already left, and he said you must dress and get your documents and run out. Go to Tumen, I'll send your effects there."

"They" was enough for me. I was all ready in two minutes, put all of my money and jewelry in my hip pockets, assumed the aspect of a wounded soldier and walked out. I barely reached Miasnitskaya Street before an armored car full of working men and soldiers passed by at about fifty miles an hour. Half a dozen bad faces looked at me. I decided to continue calmly on my way, but I heard the car coming back very soon sounding its siren. It stopped near me. "Come in, cavalry man, there is a seat for one. They found somebody in Yousupov's house."

I stopped and scratched my neck. "It cannot be done, I am going to the hospital. If I am late, I won't have the bandage changed today. Could you take me to the hospital on the Devitche Pole?"

"Are you crazy?" said the man at the wheel, looking at me with fury. "Comrades, do you think I am going to drive so far for his rotten wound?" and without asking for his friends' consent, he turned the machine and continued on his way towards Yousupov's.

This was my first interview with Russia's rulers.

23

I was stopped four or five times on my way to Deviche Pole. I took this route just to show those that might have watched me that I really was going to the hospital. Then I thought I could take a street car to a station and go somewhere south, to Tula, for instance, then wait there for a while and afterwards reach Moscow again (they cannot keep on shooting and shooting always, I reasoned) and thence to Tumen. So I continued along Miasnitskaya. Near the Post Office some people approached me. "Where to?" they asked, and a woman caught me by the arm. I made a suffering face. "For Christ's sake," I exclaimed, "don't touch me. I am wounded!" They let me go and stopped a long, young fellow in student's uniform. I saw them drag the chap away regardless of his protests. "Comrades! It is a mistake! I am a member of a local committee...." he attempted to protest,--but the woman said he looked like a suspicious plotter and they all disappeared in a side street. Near Milutinsky a man in the cap of a chauffer stopped me again and asked me to follow him. "Where?" I asked, but he did not reply and invited me to follow with a slight and nothing-good-promising-smile. "Follow!" he said.

Near a small church, there was a hardware store which we entered. About ten people were sitting on the counter. Among them were three street girls, if I might judge by their appearance and manners. Without saying a word, they all came near me, two men got me by the shoulders, two others by the legs, and in one second, my pockets were emptied, my diamonds went to the girls and a formidable blow on the spine with the butt of a rifle threw me out onto the street. "If you report," I heard a voice,--"You won't be able to count your bones."

That was really too much! All they forgot to take was a handkerchief, in which I had put some money. With that I had to reach Tumen and live there!

Then I turned left and went by small streets toward the depot from which I thought trains were running to Tumen. Where this Tumen was I really did not realize. It should be somewhere east of the Ural mountains, and all I recollected was that Cheliabinsk was the place to buy a ticket. Near a large school, I think it was an Armenian school or something, I stopped to rest and see how much money I had in the handkerchief,--but as soon as I took the handkerchief out, a man of no profession came to me and asked me to help him. While, like an idiot, I tried to figure how much I could give him,--he helped himself, grabbed my all and ran. All I could do was to send him a few greetings in my best Russian, recollecting the sins of his Mother. That relieved me, of course, but only as a palliative. I sat down near a door to think over my situation. Again a motor passed and again someone asked me who I was. I showed this time such a realistic indifference and such a display of pure disgust with life, that the man at the wheel inquired what was the matter. "Nothing, you beasts," I replied, "but that some of your own scoundrels robbed me right now." "Get after him," I continued, "perhaps you can rob him in your turn." I thought they would shoot me; nothing of the kind--they became almost sympathetic, and only asked how the man looked and which way he had gone. "Hardware store," I said, "around the corner."

24

It was Saturday night when finally our train reached Tumen: a voyage of eleven days by rail, by snow sledge, by foot, and again by rail, was at an end. God! What a sojourn, what people, what disorder! People full of onions, parasites, wounds, dirt, misery and fear! But still, in all of their misery, amiable and sympathetic, at first always desirous of helping the other fellow. Saturday night, and the church bells were ringing sadly, desperately, as if they knew nobody would come and pray. To whom? God had proved to be so far away from these people....

(pages missing)

... The city,--and I shall continue to call it a city,--was dark and dreary, and so cold that I resolved to spend the night at the depot where it was warm at least. I bought some hot tea and a large loaf of bread at the buffet, and, as a sick and poor soldier who knows his place, I sat in a corner.

There were some people in the station--mostly peasants, one could easily recognize such in them; quietly talking and drinking tea with dignity and care and biting their sugar with the force of explosions. They never put their sugar into the tea-tumblers. Later a man with a disagreeable face entered the room and looked around. This was not a peasant, I said to myself,--he would not take off his hat. The newcomer was evidently looking for me, as when he noticed me, he first bought some tea and a sandwich, and then, as if there were no other place in the room, picked out a seat near me. "An enemy," I thought to myself and buried my face in my supper.

The man wanted to talk, but evidently felt embarrassed.

"Cold outside, isn't it?" he asked.

A foreign intonation. No accent, however. A Pole or a Russian-German.

"Hm, hm, very!"

"Yes, severe climate, dog's cold. Going to stay in Tumen, or plan to go further?" he asked after a pause.

"Going to stay, or going further,--what do you ask for? But if it interests you--going to stay for a while. If I croak here, or somewhere else--you aren't going to attend my funeral. So what's the big idea?"

"Oh, nothing, nothing! You see I am a stranger here and lately live practically at the depot. Am looking for a man by the name of Vysotsky, so I ask almost everybody for the man."

"Vysotsky?" I asked, assuming an air of astonishment, "Vysotsky?" (Marchenko and his crowd flashed through my mind, especially in connection with my mission)--"no, I don't think that I know anyone by that name."

"Here, here," the man laughed, shoving me with his shoulder, "lay it out, old man, you must know him"

"No, Comrade" I responded. "You probably take me for some one else, indeed. I am Syvorotka of the 7th Hussars. We had a man by name Vysotsky, a sub-lieutenant, but I don't think it's the one you are looking for: the Vysotsky I knew has been taken prisoner, at Lvov, or at the Sziget Pass ... yes, at Sziget Pass, of course. Vysotsky, Vysotsky, what was the Christian name, perhaps that would help me out?"

"You white-collared trash!" my man suddenly became angry, "you can't fool me about his first name. Don't be too slick. I'll tell you" (he started to whisper very low and knocked on the table with his finger) "they will jail you right now, if you don't tell me why in the devil's name you came here. Aren't you going to tell me? No? Very well, I'll fix you for life, you damned Russian swine! Hope you'll choke on your tea!"

That's how he ended his friendly wishes, and left me in a fury.

But when someone threatens and is in a fury there is no immediate danger, I know. It is true in every case of life. So I was quiet for the night. I put my overcoat under my head and slept all night.

Next morning I began to work ... (several pages missing.)

25

(First letter to M. Goroshkin)

"Madame L. obtained from the Princess G-n some particulars. So in addition to the reports forwarded to you through Hatzkelman, I herewith send you more:

The Tsar's family arrived in Tobolsk from Tumen on the S/S "Russ" September 3rd, together with SS/SS "Kitai" and "Petrograd." On the last two were the accompanying persons and the "Detachment of Special Destination," with Col. Kobylinsky in command, and Mr. Makarov supervising the voyage.... For three days the "Russ" was lying near the pier, for the Governor's Mansion was not yet ready for occupancy. So nobody was allowed to go ashore. During these days crowds of people were assembled near the piers, and though in the mob there were certain evil agitators, the people in general were sympathetic, understanding the exile as a "dreadful plot of Ministers against the Emperor." The Heir was the center of the attention of the Tobolians, and his personality was not at all blasphemed.

The Emperor and the Empress, with the children, were finally put in the Mansion,--by the way its name is now "The Home of Liberty," which is on the main street of Tobolsk,--the Great Piatnitzkaya, also renamed now into Liberty Street.

The Governor's Mansion is a three-story stone house, white, with a big entrance hall from Tuliatskaya Street, there is not any entrance from Liberty Street. There is a small square place before the entrance. Here they built up a fence, not very high. They fixed the fence so that no one can go over it, as the boards are trimmed sharp and have nails. All the windows look onto Liberty Street. On the opposite side of Liberty Street are private houses. Right across the street is the house of Kornilov Brothers, also a stone building; three stories, and in this house are those who went with the family in exile.

There are sentinels around. On Tuliatskaya Street near the fence--at its ends and in the middle,--three soldiers, on Liberty Street--four soldiers; two soldiers near the entrance hall.

Though the entrance is fenced, one can see the street from the house, also from the street one can see what is going on on the stairway.

In the Kornilov House (both Kornilovs are away) are living: Dr. Botkin with his son Gleb and Miss Botkin; Dr. Derevenko--a man with the same name as the tutor of Alexis; Monsieur Gillard, a Swiss instructor of the Hier; Captain Melnik (I heard that he is going to marry M-elle Botkin); Lady-in-waiting Countess G.; M-me Schneider and several others; I shall give you their names in my next letter.

The Emperor and the Empress used to have certain liberties, they could even go to church. But then no one was admitted there, unless they could get in under the pretext of being singers in the choir. Many were going,--used to go to the Anunciation Church. They would put soldiers all of the way from the Mansion to the Church. Reports are coming that these church parades are stopped and a chapel is being built in the Mansion.

Shortly after their arrival, Mr. Kerensky sent two boxes of wine to the Tsar; the soldiers broke the boxes. They do not want any "luxuries" for the exiles. The Empress has no coffee--it is a luxury. But otherwise the attitude is not too bad. M. wrote that under the charming manners of the Tsar and especially the Heir, before the Soviet rule came, the soldiers very often changed their manners, their revolutionary hearts were melting--and then Col. Kobylinsky used to send those "soft rags" back to Petrograd, for they might be counter-revolutionary.

Kobylinsky himself was trying to maintain good relations with the soldiers, with Kerensky (who promised him promotion) and with the family through Kornilov's House, for the Emperor, like everybody else in Tobolsk, despises him. The Emperor has never said anything to or about Kobylinsky directly, however. Once only, when Kobylinsky was changing sentinels he bumped into the Emperor, and the latter said' "Still a Colonel?" That was really a sarcastic remark! Of course, now with the Bolshevik! everything has changed and the Family's position is very bad.

I am well, send me some very thick socks if you happen to have an opportunity. Greetings. Attached--a map of Tobolsk.

Yours,

Al. Syv."

(several pages missing)

26

When I returned from the Princess, tired and worried about the absence of news from Moscow and about the whole "organization" so badly and unsystematically managed, I found a dark figure sitting on my bed. A woman was attempting to light a candle. But even before I understood who was on my bed, the odor of a woman, fine perfume, burned hair and soap--struck me very strongly. I had quite forgotten during all this time of hardships this side and these agreeable ingredients of civilized life. I took my pistol, closed the door, and always sharply following the movements of the dark figure, approached her, pointing the Browning. She put her hands up.

When I finally saw the woman,--I almost fainted: it was the Baroness B., friend or enemy, but she.

She did not recognize me at first. Then:

"For God's sake!" she muttered, as if to herself, and swallowing the words, "you are Syvorotka? My God, what a horror!... How are you?"

"Madame," I said, kissing her hand,--"it certainly is a surprise,--I hope for both of us! How can I explain your presence here? Who and what brought you here?"

"It does not matter--they went away," she answered. She was looking at me with wide-open eyes, in which I noticed the sincerest amazement, if not stupefaction. "Syvorotka, you! How perfectly crazy you look with this beard! If you only knew!" and silvery laughter unexpectedly sounded in my poor quarters--in this place of mourning and sorrow--for the first time since I have come here.

"Oh, you must shave it!"

"Let my beard alone, pray," I said. "It really is not the time for any personal remarks. Besides--look at yourself; there is more paint on your cheeks than flesh. And this wig! To tell the truth I like your own hair far better. Your wig is outrageous. You look like a bad girl."

"Exactly. That's what I am now. Lucie de Clive, Monsieur, a vaudeville actress. That's me."

"A nice party, isn't it?" she said. "Syvorotka and Lucie?" "But--tell me before everything else, can I stay here?"

"Stay here? Pardon me, Baroness...."

"Call me Lucie, please...."

"Pardon me, Lucie, but really I don't quite comprehend. In these times, of course, everything has changed; but still I wish I could understand it correctly...."

"Oh, yes, you will not be bad to a poor girl, Alex, will you? I simply have to stay here--I have no other place to go."

To show her resoluteness, she took off her shabby overcoat and started to arrange her belongings, an impossible suitcase and something heavy rolled in a yellow and red blanket, looking to me from time to time with curiosity and doubt.

"Lucie de Clive! A woman certainly could not think of anything less snobbish even in these circumstances. You look like a real Russian Katka-Chort in this outfit."

"That's what is required. How did you happen to pick out your name?"

We both laughed. Indeed, if our meeting were compared to all the luxury and brilliance of the Cote d'Azur, or Petrograd--it was laughable. "Have we anything to eat?" she asked.

"I came home for my supper," I said. "I have some trash in the pantry."

While I was preparing in the so-called kitchen something nice out of a piece of frozen pilmeni--hashed meat and an old can of sardines (my pride) she began to arrange the room. She acted as if she were trying to justify her presence, it was clear. But with all the pleasure of seeing someone around my house, I simply could not think what had happened to her. Baroness B.--a lady who would not hesitate in olden times to play a thousand pounds on a horse or order ten dresses at Paquin's,-- here, asking my hospitality! If she were a Russian--I could understand it,--wives of Privy Counsellors and Ambassadors are selling cheese in Petrograd now. But she--a Foreign Lady?... It was clear, she was in some intrigue as usual, and it had led her too far.

Possibly she is after me.... And besides--her very presence would affect my work, and endanger myself. "I must give her something to eat, and then get out of here. The L. would keep me for a while, and then I shall go away. Let her stay in this house with all of her strange intrigues, for I cannot throw her out."

Thus trying to understand, I finished my cooking and asked her to the salle-amanger --the same little kitchen.

But no matter how proud I felt of my housekeeping, the Baroness found fault with everything. "Don't we have a table cloth? Or napkins? What are these daggers for?"

"Good God, Syvorotka," she said, "we ***cannot live in such a miserable way. I'll have to change it. There are no reasons why*** we should revert to cannibalism!"

Talking in that manner, jumping from one subject to another and always very nervously, she arranged the table more or less decently, and even put the salt in the lid of a little powder box. "Now," she said, "I want you to wash your hands, and comb your hair, and brush your khaki, and ..." until I got almost civilized.

When we were through with the meal and a half of bottle of beer (they call "beer" this indecent looking beverage in Tumen) I asked her what brought her to Tumen?

She told me some story--of which I believed only the fact that she was here, in my house, and that a great embarrassment had fallen on my shoulders.

"I'm glad," I said, "you did not change at all, Lucie. It is just as true--all this story of yours, as the one you told me in Petrograd. But I have no use for reforming you. Now--take me as an example of sincerity: in me, my dear lady, you see now, nothing but a poor man in hiding. All for me is in the past.... And you,--I see it--are still plotting, nothing could persuade me that you and I are here by mere coincidence. You come to me--have time to curl your hair--and you even don't tell me whether your intrigue could reveal my existence to those that persecute me. You wouldn't hesitate to pass over my dead body--for the sake of your affairs.... Again,--please do not feel offended,--there is another side. I am a working man. Tomorrow I must be at my job early in the morning. The night is growing old. So, regardless of other things,--what would you advise me to do now?"

"I have nothing to say," she answered sadly and in a low voice, "You are the Lord here."

"What do you advise me to do?" I repeated growing angry.

"I'll do anything you say," she answered blushing and lowering her head, "I am ready."

"Lucie," I said, "It is not a question of that. You see I cannot put you out on the streets. A good master would not do it to his dog. But, on the other hand they have not yet built the Ritz here."

"I am not asking you to go from your house, Alex. I had for a moment,--when I saw who Syvorotka was--a little ray of sunshine. I see I am mistaken. Could you take me to the depot, then?"

"I shall do nothing of the kind," I answered. "Nobody warned me you might come here. I was not ready. So--please stay here for to-night. I have a place where I can find an abode, and tomorrow we can decide what to do. There is some frozen milk in the pantry and if I don't return--right where you are sitting in the mattress there is some money. Good night, Lucie."

"Alex, are you really going?" she asked taking me by the arm, "Are you really going out just not to be with me? Is it a pose? Or are you serious? Please don't do it...."

"Good night," I said and went out.

27

A night in a small city of Siberia! One can see only because the snow is white. No moon, no electricity.... Where is my new Peugeot now? Who is driving it now? Where is Anton? Whose chauffer is he now, and is he still a chauffer, or has the wheel of fortune turned and made him Commissary of Arts, or Commissary of Public Health? Or, true to his master, was he hanged defending my automobile? Kismet!...

There were only two blocks to the L.--but the snow was so deep and it was so windy and cold, it seemed to me a good mile, till I reached the house.

It was dark as usual. As usual it seemed dead. But, when I was quite close to it, I heard some movement inside and I detected something in the yard. This something materialized very soon into a couple of evil faces and rifles with fixed bayonets. Inside of the house there were muffled voices. Near the rear gate (I could see it due to the sloping of the lot) three horses and a snow sledge were standing. A few voices were raised in dispute in the barn, swearing a blue streak. "Arrest"--it was clear. When I was trying to think of something to help,--and what could I think of?--the double pane of the bedroom window was suddenly broken by something heavy thrown from the inside and a desperate piercing voice of Pasha--I immediately knew it was the poor girl--shouted with all of the strength of her lungs: "Help, help! In Christ's name, help...." The cry was broken off in the middle, muffled by the palm of a hand, and became a mutter of despair and horror: "M-p-p, maa...." Somebody stuffed a white pillow in the hole. Again all became quiet.

Then the front door suddenly opened and a man jumped out into the street; another,--a short fellow clad in a wild Siberian overcoat,--appeared on the stairs, aimed a Mauser and fired at the man's back. I scarcely had time to sit down behind the fence.

Ff ... ap ... Ff ... ap ...--sounded two dry, sharp shots. The first man took two more steps--and rolled in the snow, feebly groaning from pain. A black trickle of blood swiftly ran along the snow near my knees. The Siberian overcoat looked at his victim and with "you, damned carrion," slammed the door. Again all was dark and silent.

The man was indeed dead when I reached him. He had a package of something wrapped in paper--so I took it,--I thought it might be something belonging to Ls.

All that was pretty bad, and I did not know how to get away,--my position being really a poor one in a strategic sense of the word. I had to escape without attracting too much attention. When I was thinking over how to do it--a voice called:

"Bist du dort, Swartz?"

"Ja wohl!" I answered as nonchalantly as I could, having covered my mouth with my glove, "soll' ich noch warten?"

"We'll be through in a minute. Wait a while!"

I did not wait. Through wind and snow, crawling like an Indian, I passed the dangerous spot near the gate where I could be seen, then hurried home, almost crying for the poor Ls., and Pasha--such a sweet girl, probably at that moment being nationalized--condemning all and everything and especially the impossibility of helping my unfortunate friends. All was frozen inside of me, due to the cold and this fear of a helpless creature.

When I was about a score of yards from the house--shooting started behind me--just as idiotic as in Petrograd or Moscow: in every direction, bullets cracking the windows, the street lamps, the passers-by,--on this occasion myself,--I got a bad one in the sleeve, right near the elbow.

I did not have to knock at the door as I feared running home: the door flew open, and Lucie dragged me in, closing the door behind me on the lever.

"Oh, I am so glad you came! Silly man! Are you wounded? No? I heard it all--I was so afraid that they had shot you! I am so glad, Alex dear! Do stay here, I won't be in your way, honest. Please do stay!..."

(pages missing)

28

(Second letter to M. Goroshkin)

"I must bring to your attention the fact that a certain lady, whom I knew in Petrograd in other days, came here quite unexpectedly, under the name of Lucie de Clive. She was in the plot in June, and at that time was very strongly protected by A.F. K-y, who released her from jail. She is an Englishwoman, but knows Russia well, as in fact, she knows all European countries. She came here the day the L's were killed and Pasha taken away. She made me understand that she is in a new plot to save the Emperor's family. Her task will be to stay here for a while "and make some preparations" and then go farther on.

I must tell you that her arrival here is of great inconvenience to me: in a city like Tumen it became known to the G-ns, and, though the Princess thinks I am nothing much and her morals are not for my class of people, she is a little hypocrite and pulls a long face at me.

I tried my best to avoid having this lady in my house; but the president of the local soviet, who has a great respect for me as Marchenko's protege, allowed me a short stay for the lady; I explained to him that she is my old affinity--"a civil wife." Therefore, he found it a sufficient reason, but did not like it much, and I am afraid his trust in me may diminish.

Now things have turned out in such a manner that I cannot possibly throw the lady out of my home: but what I want you to do is to notify me at once whether you know something about this arrival and whether Lucie is working for the same purposes. I don't trust her much; she feels it, and plays a strange game with me, the part of an enamored woman. This does not interfere with her writing (and receiving) some correspondence. She takes the letters out when I am busy, so I cannot trail her. I'd rather go away from here, leaving her; I would not care much to be obliged to watch her. There are certain ethics which would prevent me from liking to trail this particular lady.

I was greatly surprised when I heard that Mr. Kerensky was living in the Rossia Insurance Company Apartments, Pushkarskaya 59, Flat 10. If so, why this game of the Smolny crowd? Why not take him? The man of whom I wrote you in my last letter states that K-y is now planning to go to Stockholm and that a passport will be given to him by the Smolny Institute. Please communicate that to Marchenko. Schmelin says it is not his business. The ring was taken from K-y. Nothing new in Tobolsk. The Empress has been sick for the last ten days.

Yours,
Alex. Syv."

29

(Third letter to M. Goroshkin)

"As I told you in one of my letters, the actions of some people in Tobolsk are more or less significant.

Father A. Vassiliev has become welcome to the Emperor and has all of his confidence. We tried to warn him of this pope, but I don't think it worked, for they know that Vassiliev received some very important documents from the Emperor, and also his revolver and sword for safekeeping.

At present there is an organization in Tobolsk helping the family with money and food; the Ordovsky-Tanaevskys, the Prince Khovansky's family and the Budischevs. The latter house is on Rojestvensky Street about four blocks from the Mansion. Bishop Hermogen comes often, as well as Bishop Irinarch and some others. None are really good. The Empress is sick--the same old nervousness. The Heir is all right, barring a little accident--he fell down stairs and got a bad bump on his head. They say that the Bishop received a letter from the Dowager Empress which was brought by a German war prisoner. Others think that this letter was an act "de provocation" and has been fabricated by the Bolsheviki to circulate a bad story about the Bishop.

They speak a great deal about taking the Emperor from here to European Russia and the whole family is scared.

The situation is very precarious: there is a decided tendency on the side of the Bolsheviki to take the family away--some say, to Ekaterinburg, others to Berezov; deputies from Petrograd and Ekaterinburg, arrived in Tobolsk asking the local soviet to give up the family. The members of the "Detachment of Special Destination" do not allow that, saying that the Family will be given only to the Constituent Assembly and the population is on the side of this detachment. There may be an outbreak. In certain houses there are firearms. The situation would be better if the soldiers from the detachment had been paid; but since last September they have not been, so discontent is growing. Colonel Kobylinsky's behavior seems to be strange.

The Ufa movement is gaining in strength.

Yours,

Al. Syv."

30

(Fourth letter to M. Goroshkin)

"In case you would like to eliminate the work of my companion,--let me know, and it could be very easily done: she could be taken out of the house and put on the train going in any direction. Schmelin would help in this case. Then I would go away, for instance to Ekaterinburg or Omsk. I shall wait for your letter in regard to this, and in the meantime I'll remain just as I am now. Please do not let me stay in my actual position. I simply refuse to be aiming at her back with a concealed dagger. Even as it is, my life is untenable--the way I live, and the people I have to meet, make it perfectly horrid...."

(end of letter missing)

31

I never knew that a wireless apparatus for a range of more than one hundred miles could be such a small thing. Really this war has brought about some wonders, and it is clear to me this particular station, that was delivered yesterday, is a military outfit. I remember little about wireless telegraphy; only few explanations given to me by Capt. Volkhovsky, and after the very solemn inauguration of the "Spark-Radio" we had a gala-performance. It is but a superficial study indeed.

I cannot understand this strange silence of Goroshkin. Is he dead? If he is dead--what happened to Marchenko? Are they both dead? Now since the Ls are gone and Pasha has become some Bolshevik's property (poor little thing!) I have no idea what to do. Shall I consider myself in the game, or did the whole organization end; shall I continue on my own behalf? I have been thinking, and thinking about it, and have decided that I must continue my informative functions, and must wait as I have been told. They said I shall be on my post--and I must remain. The absence of letters does not mean much: they can be in a terrible situation in Moscow now--we know nothing. If my letters have not reached Goroshkin--they have reached somebody else; in the latter case I would have been hanged long ago, or shot, or something similar, if the letters did not reach friends.

Lucie? Well if she is not the crookedest woman! I do not think I could get rid of her now even if I would. Schmelin knows of my going out of town, it is clear. Of course he closes his eyes,--but I never can doubt that he will be the first to "put me on a clear water" as soon as he apprehends that the other commissaries know of my wanderings and trading with the Letts, and of what is now under our bed.

Something new: Lucie received a rubber bath, so I have to warm up the water and then wait....

(end of page missing)

... She would come back, as soon as I shall be ready putting the wires instead of the ropes in the yard for drying the linen. I was glad to know it. Certainly. Personally I am very glad to see her around: she is a nice little woman when she does not plot. It is agreeable to have tea at five and then everything looks so clean and neat since she came. Good God, should she be simply a nice little Lucie! How agreeable everything could become--as if there were no Revolution, no Bolsheviki, no Emperor.... But no; Fate has to put a drop of tar in a barrel of honey. However, perhaps I would have hated to see a cook around here: as soon as a woman gets too domestic--she infallibly becomes unattractive. As for Lucie--enclosed in a cage as we are--I never saw her unwashed, uncombed, frivolous or unladylike. So let her be a plotter. I must be grateful as we never quarrel.... She sends me away when....

(end of page missing)

32

(Fifth letter to M. Goroshkin)

"... a man by name Alexander Petrovich Mamaev from Novo-Nikolaevsk. He has a plan of his own, which he wants to accomplish. He has some people working for him, nothing serious, if I may judge. Mamaev's plan is being worked out this way: his people will buy out the sentinels and take the Emperor and the Heir (perhaps the Princesses, but, as he says "the old woman will never be considered") and rush both eastward by the old highway. On the stations Mamaev's people are now hiring horses and coachmen. They have collected money amongst the merchants. They plan to take the Emperor as far as Blagoveshchensk-on-Amur. Thence to San-Haliang, on the Chinese side of the river. From San-Haliang somewhere out of the country,--I never heard where to. The organization works successfully in the region of Tomsk, where all is ready for immediate action.

There is much imagination in Mamaev's plan, and though I know his preparations are watched in Ekaterinburg, they do not meet with approval at all. Captain Kaidalov of the Crimea Horse Regt. is now the soul of Ekaterinburg and he does not approve. He is a fine fellow, I know, and very courageous: he went to the local soviet, became their confident and *persona grata* and I think is virtually the only one who really understands the problems and realizes their difficulty and their danger. Please let me know whether I should inquire any longer about all of this!

Yours,
Alex. Syv."

33

Sunday she came back from the trip. I felt quite lonesome all of this week. Two men were with her: one--a Russian, the silent type, with a big hat, who was taking care of the horse: the other, a tall, broad faced Anglo-Saxon fellow, whose bronzed face would be appropriate in the tropics but not on the white steppes of Siberia. A little longhaired pony brought the trio in a fancy sledge early in the morning. The Englishman (his name is Stanley) started to work with the radio, silent, serious, smoking a short black pipe. He took me for Lucie's servant. If I had had any doubt of his nationality, I never could have mistaken his tobacco: Navy Cut,-- the one make I can't tolerate. He filled our small house with blue clouds of stink. When they all came I ran to the sledge, but from a distance Lucie signaled to me with her eyes that no tender expressions were needed. She sent me out for food, then to a drug store, then to the post-office, etc., etc. I obeyed.

So around noon I went to see the Princess. They all make me sick, especially since the L. tragedy. "If God does not help--we cannot." A certain Mme. K-v is now hanging around her. A suffragette--that's what she is. She said "some women are now here--we know nothing about ..." alluding of course to me. I hardly could wait until evening.

It was evening when S. finished connecting the kitchen station with the city current. When I came home he and the Russian were trying to harness the pony. The poor little horse was choking from the smoke of his pipe and trying to bite the torturer.

"Say, Lucie," the Englishman said to her, as shivering in my overcoat, she came out to say good-bye to him, "the benzine is in the barn, over there under the hay. Tell your man to be careful and not to smoke around here."

"If it did not explode after your pipe, sir," I replied in my best Shakespearian, "my cigarette won't do any harm. So don't be alarmed."

It took him about half a minute to digest the fact that I could understand his cockney. Lucie became almost hysterical with laughter and ran into the house.

Then he made a serious face and sprang into the sledge and the Russian flicked the horse with the whip. Near the corner, I saw him say something to the Russian and they turned back.

"Say," the Englishman asked, "are you English? Or Canadian, I fancy?"

"Never mind me, Major or Captain, or whoever you are. I'm just I. Don't fancy, and proceed. I'm busy."

I closed the gate and heard another formidable crack of the whip on the pony's fat flanks.

Hundreds of bells started ringing again, and then died away in the distance, drowned out by a locomotive whistle....

And here I was in my room again. In the corner stood Lucie, lovely creature with all her funny actions and thoughts, Heaven knows by what and whom inspired.

"Look what I brought, Alex! Here are canned goods, and chocolate and coffee, and ham, and ..." and she threw package after package on the bed. On one of them I read "Army and Navy Calcutta," but said nothing and looked away. I'm getting sly. She noticed it too, the little devil! She sent me out to see whether or not the gate was closed, and when I came back the label was scratched out.

34

(Sixth letter to M. Goroshkin)

"There are, virtually, three--or perhaps more--organizations, members of which have decided to save the Emperor from imprisonment. They all realize the danger of letting things go on by themselves, or of relying upon German promises.

The latter are well known here and in Tobolsk from Bolshevik sources. When during the Brest-Litovsk pourparlers the Russian Delegates were waiting for the Germans, the latter entered the room of conference, and found it filthy with smoke; the Bolsheviki were extremely hilarious, and laughed and joked among themselves. To show his independence Monsieur Trotsky was sitting on the table; others were without collars and in the most unrespectable state of humor. When the German delegation entered they did not move; the leader of the Germans, an old general, stopped for a moment, looked at them in disgust, and then suddenly shouted:

"Stand! Attention! Get up, you, Kameraden!"

Electrified--they all got up, Trotsky first, although with the remark "For why"? The General continued:

"By order of His Majesty the King and Emperor, I declare that there is at To-bolsk in your hands the relative of my August Master,--Her Imperial Majesty the Empress of Russia with her consort and children. Until this is arranged--we shall not proceed with this conference of ours. We demand your guarantees that 1st--you vouch for their perfect safety; 2d--you immediately will take steps to deliver the prisoners abroad. Now, at rest! Sit down!"

I was told that the delegates from the soviets had the authority to vouch for them in this regard, for they say unofficially that the matter had been previously taken up by Russian and German diplomacy. So a telegram was sent by Joffe to Lenine, who answered, "measures taken." Then the Brest-Litovsk sale commenced.

This evidently was not fulfilled, although I have heard that there is certain movement on the part of Germans, especially amongst the war prisoners. I consider it impracticable. At present the military situation is as follows: the Czechs are nearing the Samara-Zlatoust line; in Siberia--there is a very big movement of Czech war prisoners and Russians--to assist the Czechs in their task of reaching the Pacific. Battles are raging on the Volga front. It is evident that the salvation of the Family cannot come from Germany, for there would not be any place and way to take the Emperor out of Tobolsk, but by way of the Trans-Siberian,--a long journey with no possibilities of getting out of this country. The local Bolsheviki are beyond the control of the centers. They want to "govern" themselves--evidently with no orders and particularly confidential (I think this one would be such) would not be executed.

The Ekaterinburg organization is weak as I already wrote you. First because the organization is in Ekaterinburg and the Emperor in Tobolsk.

Who are these people? They want first of all, and altogether, restitution for the sake of getting good positions for valuable services rendered the Family. They all see that the restitution is problematic,--so their desire is not strong. They act weakly, they think lazily, they move with an agony of indifference. All that they have done is certainly known to Kobylinsky and--to the Commissaries. And if they are not yet all arrested--it is because the sovietists want to know their actions. If the damned lack of organization, that we all are suffering from, can be noticed in our present life--it is ideally clearly seen in the Ekaterinburg circles. The Princess G. and others are of the same sort; dully thinking, believing in and hoping for marvels and miracles, trying to look busy and tired. They gossip about each other, they are ready to sink each other in a spoonful of water. Now what is their plan? They haven't any,--at least, nothing definite. They all say vaguely "we are going to buy out Col. Kobylinsky and the sentinels and the Bolsheviki." All right. Supposing there were someone among them who would go and try this buying proposition? Supposing they were to buy Kobylinsky, and the sentinels and the Bolsheviki. What will they do with the Emperor? Against them there would be the whole world. There is no way for the Ekaterinburg people to get him out, just as there is no way for the Germans. All is closed for them, except a crazy scheme of taking the Family into the interior, which I do not consider feasible. It is impossible. I was told to watch all that I could in connection with the move in Tumen; I was instructed to watch the Ekaterinburg organization and the Princess. I hope I am not considered a member of this organization as it is a failure, and I hate to participate in deadborn adventures.

Again there is the work that Lucie is doing. I do not know for whom she works, though I can see she is not working by herself. I can see that there is 1st, a certain participation of people with means--she has money and certain buying capacities, a sign of great importance at present: 2d, there is evidently a planned and systematic scheme of work in all the actions around me; 3d, there is an unseen hand directing the whole enterprise, decisive and strong.

What is this plan? I can as now see only one thing: provisions are made, both in food and munitions, and shipped through my home east. There is an intense wireless communication--I cannot know what it is about. A man in smoked glasses comes every evening and sits--near the apparatus. Sometimes he only listens in; sometimes he gets his "tune" and talks. In the latter case, Lucie goes down town and leaves me at home. I think she mails the communications or maybe someone waits for her in the post office, or, what is possible....

(few lines scratched out)

... Her Russian is not at all good, she hardly speaks it in fact, but she gets along as Lucie de Clive, a French demoiselle. With her, as far as I can see are the following elements: 1st, the British officer,--Stanley, or whatever his name really is; 2d, the silent Russian, with wiry Siberian hat and extremely profane language (I think he swears when praying): 3d, two Letts as she calls them, though there is just as much Lettish in them as in you, or me,--they both speak Russian like Russians; 4th, myself. About the last point I can tell, that lately I am in the traffic business. Lucie asks me very often to take loads to the outskirts of Tumen, near the Freight Depot, which we receive with the Siberian pony, and I take it in my sledge behind the Depot, where I deliver the goods--only in the evenings--to the Letts. Sometimes we speak, but never much.

Usually, "Very cold," or "How snowy," or "Have you a cigarette?" After delivering the goods--altogether I have done it about five times, I return home. The Letts wait to move until I go away; I did not succeed in trailing them--and honestly would not want to very much. I have my private reasons for not getting into Lucie's way. Besides, why should I? I am sure that we all are working for the same purpose, but perhaps from different standpoints. On the other hand, it astonishes me exceedingly, that Lucie....

(two lines scratched out)

and he arranged for my protection and undisturbed life here,--so seemingly everything is in perfect accordance. You never answer my letters, but couldn't you manage to acknowledge them? Please do it.

Yours,

Alex. Syv."

35

"I have been here so long!... Isn't it funny, Alex, how the time has passed?"

The night was a windy one as though Winter knew it was its last chance to freeze people to death before Spring would come; the long night seemed slow in coming. All day we had worked very hard in the barn preparing a big load which Lucie had asked me to take to the Letts. After dinner, we had kippered herring and some meat stew a l'Irlandaise, we were sitting near the open oven. "Lent bells! I wonder who is praying?..."

"Yes, six weeks, dear. Six weeks of perfect sincerity and mutual trust,--it is not a little thing."

She accepted my remark without turning her face from the fire near which we were sitting. "Six weeks," she said again.

"Do you remember the man who was playing near me in Monte Carlo the day we met?"

"There were too many of them. Which one do you mean?"

"The tall man, Mr. Osborne--never mind trying, it does not matter, I just happened to think of him."

"Anything identical with our six weeks of life?" I asked, and immediately regretted my bad temper--I am getting impossible.

"Very much," she said sadly. "Very much; only under other circumstances, other climates, other people. Not so inconsiderate."

When I looked at her my heart filled with pity. Who is this woman? I don't know her. Perhaps she has something in her heart--the very existence of which I had oftentimes doubted. Perhaps, in her life of adventures, she has had more hardships, more of tragedy than I,--with all of my selfish sufferings of a man who used to be rich and prominent, and is now humble and poor? Perhaps she has more of self-control not to show it,--nevertheless the amount of her bitterness of life must be the same, if not deeper, than mine?

We have been here for six weeks.... I have no place to go. So I am here. But she? I am sure she could be somewhere else, in better surroundings, amongst people better than I am. And during these six weeks--we were not friends. We were only plotters, joined under one roof, and secretly hostile to each other--"I am ashamed," I said to her, "honestly I am. You must think that I have never cared to know what is in your mind. We have always been distant and mysterious, always absorbed in our own affairs. Why should I trouble you with my questions? Especially, if I knew beforehand that you wouldn't answer. Yes, we have been together six weeks--more than that--we live under the same roof, eat the same food, have our life as close as two human beings can,--and yet--here we are,--apart from each other. You are a woman, it's up to you to break this distance and build a bridge over it."

"Well," she said, putting her small hand on mine, "you approach the question evidently from another angle. I am not speaking of our business, which may, and which may not, be the same. Why am I so sad and so blue? It is that I feel I am all alone here. I can tell you and I think that you have already understood it, that I came to Tumen with orders to see a certain Syvorotka. I had to be with him, use his house, use his protection, use his connections. I did not know who this Syvorotka was.

A cave man? An ex-soldier? A sick man? A fat butcher? A sentimental, but dirty druggist? Of all the men in the world,--and while coming here I imagined all possible types,--that I should have met you, Alex! You have always meant so much to me. I have always liked you. When I saw you last in Petrograd I tried to get you into my affairs. Why? I don't know. You have no ambitions, you have no character,--nothing. And still, I tried to get you, only to be with you. You refused--for you never cared: perhaps once in Marseilles, when you wanted to kiss me (you see I did not forget)--and even at that time you were drunk.... And here in Tumen--you were the man, with whom as they told me, I had to go as far as was necessary to get his good services...."

"Strange life, this one of mine," she ended her remark and again turned to look into the flames.

"Lucie, you never told me you cared, I thought you were for your own affairs much more than for anything else; now I see it in a different light."

"You do? It is late. I am going. I am leaving you--this time for good. A week--or so, and I am far away from here, from you--with all of your good and bad qualities. The time in which we live--does not allow any speculations. One must get what he sees."

What do you mean by 'going away'?"

"Just what I say. I received orders to move to another place. No, I cannot tell you. That's all. You, and this little house, and some hopes I had here,--all, all, must be forgotten. Other people, and other scenery. A radical change again. Heavens knows how soon I can forget this little white cold town...."

"Yes," she continued, looking at me, "yes, this cold town, with you; and you--with your double-crossings, with your reports on me, with your bad behavior, with your treason. Alex--love is a strange thing. I don't mind it at all! You never knew it. You never loved your poor Maroossia: she was your comfort--that's all. You never thought of Lucie de Clive as such: for you--she was a little girl that possibly might have been in your way, but you let her stay because she comforted you. Now--she is going, and very likely you won't see her any more. In your life--she was a page of a book; now you've read it!..."

She was crying, really crying! Such an actress!

36

I came home at seven from the village--nobody in there! Nobody to give me my tea. All looks empty, abandoned. On the bed pinned to the pillow,--a note: "Good-by." My companion left me--today. And I had so much to say to her....

She did not forget to look in my bag before leaving, as I see. I thought so.

My diary has been censored: many pages are missing and some rough hand-made corrections in the text have been made leaving greasy spots on the paper. Some of my documents are stolen. I don't see the letter from Marchenko to Schmelin, the chart with Mamaev's stations, and a few others. Fortunately, Kerensky's letter to Grimm was not taken, as I had put it under the floor of the barn with my money and watch.

She must have had the help of the man with the specs--she would not be able to understand my scratching. They must have been busy all day! But what really gets me wild--almost all of my letters to Goroshkin are here! How did she get them? I understand why Goroshkin's letters missed me--she got them!... Now I understand what she meant by saying that I was trying to double cross her! In fact Lucie is right,--and that's why it's maddening. I wonder what Goroshkin and Marchenko think of me? To whom I must seem a swine! And what a bad way of her's, to leave my letters--a present for me!

She did what she wanted, this creature of intrigues and no personality: with "lips of fire and heart of stone." She got in me a good guardian of her barn, a good transport agent for her Britishers and Letts, she tangled me up in such a way that I could not report on her, she enjoyed the privileges of local Soviet's protection through me,--in short all she wanted.... And here I am alone from now on,--Good-by"--that's all. She left me this little note--and a bitter feeling that formerly I was not alone,--and now I am. For these sensations of lonesomeness a man should never start companionships,--whether with a woman, or a dog, or even a goldfish. The one who is alone--is alone. The one that becomes alone--feels doubly rotten....

"Quidquid ages--prudenter agas, et respice finem"--and I was a fool,--here I am alone like Shelly's moon, and "pardessus-le-marche"--robbed! Am I not an old ass?

She will laugh with her silvery laughter in somebody else's house, she will mend somebody else's socks, and sit on somebody else's lap. The "other chap from Monte Carlo," will be asked whether he remembers me. And the other chap will probably answer her, as I did. How tactless!

My God! Long and uninteresting life looks to me! Does it only look, or did it become?... I must sleep all of this off!

37

My sole connection with the rest of the world is my work in the Princess' garden. A dull, tiresome, uninteresting work, in fact--labor. As a diversion--the corpulent cook. My God! If she would only wash oftener!...

When I come home--I look out of the small window; the landscape is magnificent: about twenty yards of virgin soil with Spring grass on it and the barn on the horizon. Behind--the fence, over which I see the tops of the heads of passers-by.

"Suave mari magno turbantibus aequora ventis spectare laborem...." I forget how it runs further! My latin gets weak. I wish I had Virgil, or even "Commentarii de Bello Gallico." I'd be arrested and tried if I asked for them in a book store....

If only I could obtain some money, and buy a decent suit and get away,--to Vladivostok, and then through America to France. It seems as though France is all. It is life. It is salvation from my miseries.

In the evenings I try to arrange in shape my documents and writings after the looting. For the documents I could be well paid, here,--but I do not want that. Let the Russia of to-morrow see what has been done by our present leaders, and by those who gave us to the scaffold.... M. Kerensky's letter to Grimm--alone would make me happy if some day its contents are known....

Where is Lucie now? How empty my house is!

The Princess came out to me in the garden and asked me whether I could go to

Tobolsk and deliver a letter to Mr. Botkin there.

"Of course, I can, your Ladyship, if I have enough money."

"I don't mean that," she answered coldly, looking with disgust at the manure I was mixing, "don't worry, we will pay you. I mean whether you could arrange with your Bolsheviki for a permit."

"Why not?" I answered, "they do not want me. I am not a rich man, nor a Nobleman...." (I simply love to annoy her).

"That will do, Alexei," she said, casting at me a nasty look, "You may come for the letter at dinner time. Tell the cook that you want to see me."

She does not think that I am a man. She hates me. Under my beard and shabby flannel shirt she sees neither my face nor my person. She has no shame before me: were I in my uniform of a gentleman-in-waiting, cleanly shaven and speaking her language, and not in the one I acquired lately, she would have buttoned her shoes, gartered her stockings, and would not have shown the bad quality of her corset cover under her wide-opened robe-de-chambre. If she only knew how her hired help understood her.

At four I was in the kitchen. Here--another interesting phase of life! The woman from Moscow who claims to be a cook, does not think I am from her midst, but feels with her organic cleverness that I am an imposter.

"You,--gentry! You liar! Hate your face! Hope the devil will get you soon!" she says,--but she isn't a bad woman, she means well, only she is not as clean as her profession demands. Altogether the kitchen is a mournful place.

"What is your business?" she asked, "You want to see the Princess? Don't lie to me!"

"My business is none of your business," said I, "Forget it! Better tell me if I can have some beer? Go on, cookie, lay it out. Don't be so stingy!"

The stubborn woman would not give it to me, until I took her gently around the waist and pinched her arm with all of my force,--that's the way to get cook's sympathies; it's astonishing how it works! I got some beer.

Then I was invited in: "Come in, you scabby devil."

"You will have to take this," said the Princess, giving me a letter so that she wouldn't touch my hand, "and be sure they don't catch you with the letter. Be careful, don't drink, Alexei. It's bad to drink; when you come back we'll give you 500 rubles."

"Je ne le tolere pas," she said to the Prince, "il a l'air si commun! Il nous vendrait tous, s'il etait assez intelligent!"

The Prince did not answer (I guess he knows more than her Highness) and looked aside, grumbling something just to calm his better half.

I stared at her, just to scare this bad female, from under my eyebrows.

"Vous voyez," the Princess almost cried, "Vous voyez! Mon Dieu! Quel type horrible! J'ai peur de lui! C'est un degenere! il nous trahira!" She complimented me in this manner for a while, and then started to give me some silly instructions,--how to get there, etc.

Finally, I left the house, went to Schmelin and got his permission in a minute, and tonight--I am leaving.

My house and all in it will be taken good care of,--Schmelin promised to look after it.

Good-by, my humble hut! Good-by Tumen!

III. TOBOLSK

38

The Irtysh opened its dark blue streams for navigation not so long ago. From my place on the deck I see spots of old yellowish snow on the hills; near the banks--the fresh, innocent grass is already daring to appear on the surface. Peasants are doing something on the vast plains. The very, very old story of the mythical Lei! White and chaste birches, triste and flirtatious women amongst the trees, are trimming their Spring fashion dresses.

However this coming back to life, of the hills, and plains, and trees, this warmth in the air--does not affect the passengers. Who in the devil will nowadays snivel about Spring and myths? All sentiment died in Russia; everything, at least, looks dead,--but the co-operative Societies: they plan a large business, meaning "trusts" when they advertise for "co-operation."

With the exception of the representatives of the "Creamery Union" (who were fat and noisy),--the rest of our fellow-travelers were gloomy and sordid; I rarely could detect a smile, and if there was a hilarious expression, it was at somebody's expense, always malicious and malignant. A boy cut his little finger and squealed for "mama" like a young pig--people smiled. An old woman passed on the deck and fell so badly that tears came into her colorless eyes--smiles became bright and gay; somebody even whistled. A stowaway was caught in the baggage room--a pale faced young chap with a forlorn expression--the crew committee started to "investigate" (just undressed him on the deck)--and people became joyful and gigglish....

Is it my people? Are those *bad creatures--our men who fought in the snows of Hungary armed with fists and patriotism,--for the munitions were yet the sub-*

ject of speculations; did these men cross the scorched plains of Persia, sent there clad in uniforms prepared for Archangel? Did they *make efforts to save small mutilated nations? Is the history of Russia--these pages of blood and sacrifices--* made by them? Did Russia take from them Pushkin, Chaikovsky, Mechnikov, Tolstoi and the brilliant web of savants, musicians, soldiers, explorers and poets?...

I am from this same bulk that centuries ago came from Asia and settled here. They--and I are the same. But I can't understand them! In France, in England, in Germany, I could understand the crowd better. But these men and women are so far from my conception.... And they all pay me back with the same coin: they not only misunderstand me and my kin,--but they mistrust me. I can deceive a bolshevik commissary, or the Princess G.; these--with their psychology never would let me come closer. I am an intruder to their caste.

Before--in Petrograd--we all have had this very same fear of our select caste for a newcomer, just as these have. In our midst the man who tried to break in would be caught right away. Now I understand this little, mean, reptile impulse of catering to the one whom you seek, this feeling that the parvenu must have felt, this sensation of the necessity of flattering, for which one blushes in the nights, for which one can't sleep and turns endlessly in warm cushions. The parvenu! Pushkin said:

  ... and an exchange of silent glance   Forever took away his chance....

It was enough for us to look at each other--and the parvenu would not come near us any more. Here--instead of the poetical form of Pushkin I must recollect the words of the Tumen cook:

"You liar! Hate your face of a gentry!"

Isn't it a correct translation from my Russian into theirs?

Well,--I'd rather stop my scratchings: Tobolsk.

39

"Do not write too much," said a walking corpse clad in rags, seating himself near me on a soft pack of his baggage. "It is better to forget all about it. Why do you do it? What is the use?" His suffering face was not at all familiar to me,--so, when he asked me, "Haven't we met before?"--I said No. He looked to me like one of those Siberian peasants. Then, under the coat of dirt, under his rags and an old Orenburg shawl, I really saw something familiar.

"Perhaps we met," I said. "Petrograd?"

"Yes, indeed," he bowed his old head and sighed. "I used to go very often to the French Theatre. You remember 'L'Aiglon?' Can I chat with you a bit? This silence is simply killing me. Four months of silence! Don't you think, mister writer, of what a sweet, what a wonderful word 'revenge' is? If you write--do write about it! Revenge for having cleaned the streets, for having been thrown out of every Embassy, every Legation, every Consulate--whose three sons are sleeping there, on the Prussian Frontier--forever?--when I begged them to help me and let me go to Paris only to die near my wife? Revenge! Just to see England--torn to pieces, France--robbed, Japan--licking our feet,--to see them separately doing what we suffer combinedly. They all betrayed us, they sold us, they mock at us! We are paying for our readiness to save Serbia. We are dying for it--and I do not regret it. I know that from our dead body, from our bier--poisonous flowers are growing; their fragrancy will send pestilence and destruction to our lucky Allies, and ruin them, and ruin them.... If I only could help it.... If only I could live long enough to witness it."

The man looked crazy to me. He evidently is one of those whose minds gave way. His eyes were sparkling flames--while his greenish face with a sluttish beard remained immovable and serious. From away--we both were talking of our village affairs.

He continued:

"Don't you think I am talking for myself. It is for Russia. I am finished anyhow. Go ahead! Betray me too. Tell them I am Counsellor of State, and a landlord, and marshal of nobility. I do not care! I am finished.... Yet in my better days I had cancer. It was almost a pleasure then. Don't smile, it's true. Now--I need oysters, and fruit, and fine Port wine, and medicine,--and I have bread, which I cannot digest, and they kick me out of every hospital.... I'm sure the cancer is nearing my heart. If I die,--I won't see my remuneration: the downfall of our traitors. Friend,--what can I do to hasten it? How can I avenge Russia?..."

"It is a hard question to answer. I think you exaggerate a little. I am myself after a settlement, but I do not go so far. My goal is smaller. I would like to find a man in Petrograd, so that I could make the rest of the world understand what he really is. He is a criminal cretin. Yes, it is this man, exactly. But not at this time. Look around: The Spring is here. Don't you think the air is pacifying? The air calls to a perfect selfishness. So, if I had seen the man right here, I would have shot him of course, but I hate to think of getting into trouble now."

"Air! Spring! Are you in love, young man?"

Then he grew sad and silent for a while. "No, I can't see any pleasure in Spring." He became sunk in his thoughts, and looked away.

I love Winter just because it dies every year, and gives place to a new life! And again the thin birches become green and chastely white. And I know my birch is somewhere--looking for me.

Tobolsk! Pretty town--I must admit. The high bank with green slopes is covered with churches, white buildings and gleaming gold crosses. Something tranquil about Tobolsk! Blue, red and green roofs look shy from their cozy nests of trees. It must be very exciting to live here when all is normal. Good God! I see from the deck the fine foggish veil of dust and gossips hanging over the town. They must still play "preference" here, or "vint." In these little "centers" bridge must be unknown.

I took a room in a hotel and went to the Kornilov house. It was about four. I heard the noise of forks and knives, dinner time is so impossibly early in these longitudes. A man answered my ring and said I should wait outside and never ring the front door bell. He explained where the kitchen entrance was. The man, even in explaining these disagreeable things, was polite: by profession, for I immediately saw he was a former Chamber-lackey, though he had a moustache and was looking meager. "Wait on the street, service-man," he said, "I cannot let you in." Very well,--I know these "waits" and "call later ons." They don't hurt me.

I crossed the street and went down the slope. There is a post office on the corner,--and a soldier near it,--a regular Lett: white eyebrows, red face and the meanest steel blue microscopic eyes deeply placed under a low forehead. He looked at me and impendingly changed the rifle from one shoulder to the other. I turned upwards and continued all along this "great Liberty Street." I did not want to pass near the Mansion. I turned on the Tuliatskaya, passed two blocks and explored where the Budishchevs were. Again a Lett, again no eyebrows over the same piggish eyes. And again a Lett. Gracious! One more in here--and the whole Letvia must be in Tobolsk!

When I knew the city well enough I turned back to Kornilov's.

The same chamber-lackey opened the rear door almost killing me with the smell of cabbage.

"Dr. Botkin is not in," he said, when I explained what I wanted, "Sit down, service-man. Take it"--he gave me a cigarette with a gold crescent on it--the kind they served at the Palace. I looked at the crescent and then at the man. In one glance he got I was not "service-man," but he did not show his discovery,--only got up and continued talking.

"The doctor is very busy right now. He was asked across the street twice today. Have you come from Russia? Demobilized?"

"Yes, quite demobilized," I answered. "I must see Mr. Botkin right now, so won't you please tell him about me as soon as he returns. Don't worry about the kitchen--I cannot stay here: I'd rather sit outside."

He showed me through the dining room into the front hall. From there I could see the Mansion quite well. A little square in front of it was fenced in, but not very high. On the front stairs I noticed two women and a boy, in whom, notwithstanding his torn-out shoes and unhappy looks, I recognized the unfortunate Heir to the Russian Throne. Someone called him in--and he went slowly into the house. Two Reds passed near the women smoking pipes and dragging the rifles by their bayonettes. They both looked piercingly at the women and exchanged a few words with each other. The women slowly moved toward the house. Their life must be a real torture within this fence!

A man of medium height passed from the Mansion and crossed the street. He entered the Kornilov House, and after short conversation with the chamber-lackey,--

"Did you wish to speak to me?" he asked,--I am Dr. Botkin."

"Yes, sir."

"Now,--what is it?"

"I come from Tumen, Dr. Botkin. I have brought you a letter from your friends."

A grimace passed over his face, and he stared at me with suspicion. "Tumen? Who are you?"

"I hardly think my name would tell you anything, doctor. Here is the letter."

He stopped my movement:

"Please, please, not here. Let's go in. Don't be so sure of this place."

We entered the dining room, and he took the letter and opened the envelope. After reading--there were no more than two pages--he said:

"No answer. Do you know the contents?"

"I don't. But I can guess."

"Oh! Is that so?"

All of this commenced to irritate me. I shrugged my shoulders.

"Very well, very well," the doctor said, "we must not be offended. You know what times we live in. Won't you sit down, please?"

The doctor was very nervous: rubbed his hands, looked around and showed other signs of impatience. Finally he expressed what was in his mind.

"Can't the Princess understand how risky these writings are for us?"

"Just as risky as for the authors and bearers," I replied feeling sorry for the lady who meant well. "If there is no answer I don't think I'll return to Tumen. I have nothing to do there. I see all these affairs are managed in the same way, as we managed them in our country. I am through. I thought we had changed. I'll attend to other things."

"Please," he said looking at me with amazement, "don't misunderstand me. You see,"--he tried to invent something, or say something,--"all is very dangerous...."

We were interrupted by a movement on the street. A crowd of soldiers (for I cannot call it a company, or a detachment,--just a crowd of man-haters clad in uniform) passed, and made a demonstration against the Mansion. A few stones and pieces of wood flew onto the Mansion's roof, where they landed and rolled down with a rattling noise, scaring the inhabitants. A frightened face looked out of the window--and hid immediately.

"The Hooligans!" said Botkin. "Every God's day the same, every God's day!"

With laughter and whistles the crowd went down the Great Liberty Street. All started suddenly and just as quickly ended; the street became calm again.

Botkin turned to me and continued:

"Perhaps I was too hasty about this 'no answer.' I should've said it otherwise. I think it is of no use to attempt to do anything, that's the idea. If any plan will be successful,--it will not be this," he showed the letter, "though it is appreciated, trust me when I say it! We are confronted with other interests, we happen to be in somebody's game." He wanted to add something,--but stopped. "Perhaps our misery was seen abroad through this dead screen of general selfishness! Believe me, sir, any attempt is hopeless. Our effort only spoils, or might spoil, more cleverly prearranged plans. Now--if you wish me to be frank, I personally don't believe in what I say to you. I think the song is sung...."

"Very well, if I happen to communicate, I'll say so."

An old lady passed the room and searchingly gazed at me. Then a man, tall and thin came in, got a drink of water and left. We both kept silent. An atmosphere of distrust reigned for a while. I got up.

"Wait a while," Botkin said, "I still would like to know whom I have the pleasure of speaking to?"

"Syvorotka is my name. I'll stay here in the hotel for a while."

He looked at me without any confidence.

"As you please," he said, "I cannot force you to take the mask off. Good-by."

We shook hands,--and I left the Kornilov's House.

Here I am in the Hotel. Dirty hole--that's it. No linen. A mattress covered with spots. Rotten humor.

Botkin fears that the efforts might compromise those who are around the Mansion. He fears even those who are in exile. He fears everything. But--not for himself. I think he is an honest man.

There is nothing to do here--with these scared people. Suspicious, having lost faith in each other, and jealous! I must try to approach them against their will,--perhaps I can do something better than in Tumen.

It is evident that the tragedy develops here. I would not be surprised to know that Lucie is somewhere around.

40

With my pass from the Tumen soviet and a very sure feeling of a perfect disguise, I came yesterday to the local scoundrels,--the "high commission of investigations" as they call this filthy, impossible place where they meet. It used to be the

Ecclesiastical School in other days. I had quite a time penetrating these regions guarded by the Reds. The man to whom I was recommended was an elderly kind-faced fellow. All he was saying to me was virtually addressed to the crowd of Reds in the room; as for the room, I think it used to be in former times the professors' room.

"Yes, yes,--your credentials are perfect. Comrade Schmelin,--of course I know him! You have no such troubles in Tumen as we have here. But--all must be done. And for the sake of the Revolution and the Proletariat--we are here, and will do our duty."

To show how much power he had, he gave some orders to the Reds. They would come near him to take these orders, stand still as they were standing only a few months ago before an officer, and then turn in the brusque manner of soldiers.

The kind faced man--with his sly Jewish features and bulgy big eyes, did not ask me who I was, how I was, and why I wanted the position of an "advising commissary" with the detachment. He looked at me, and smiled,--read the letter I presented,--and, seeing on my face an admiration for his splendor, accepted me. My God, how alike these people-in-power are! I remember, in my early days, the Count Witte, a man with heavy, depressing looks. He liked this move of a man-of-power. I recollect Mr. Kokovtzev who liked so much to see admiration on his visitor's face.... I see this little insignificant and blunt Kerensky, that fished for worship.... And here,--this "tovarishch" Nachman--sitting in his chair and ruling--had the same identical signs of self-respect, self-adoration, and independence. And--with all of them--I would, without any effort, just by instinct, get on their feeble side, change the whole expression of my face,--even think like them, and love them,--and win. The instinct of accommodation is a great thing,--and, it seems to me I possess it in sufficient volume.

So--accepted in the ranks of those that go wherever they wish, that do whatever their left foot feels like doing, those that continue to remodel the country, those that are so free in every action--I sat near the powerful man,--Comrade Nachman--as equal to equal.

But--what I really could not conceive,--was the range of his duties; he was judge, and governor, and military commander, and lawyer, and coroner, and administrator of the city, and the notary public--all that used to be connected with business--was his concern.... They could not do it in the olden days; they had to have a specially trained man for every branch before,--and now!

"How perfectly you perform all of these different duties," I said.

41

I am a jailer; I guess the first in our family.

Together with Comrade Adolf Pashinsky,--a Pole from the dreadnaught "Andrey Pervozvanny,"--I am walking on the Great Liberty Street, and inside of the fence, watching the prisoners in the Mansion, and watching to see that supreme justice --the will of the people--be done.

My companion--is a muscular man of thirty, without front teeth; his thin lips are always curved in a bad smile; his brain is such that he cannot think and speak of anything that would not be vulgar and vicious.

The very first night we came to change sentinels--I felt embarrassed, as I do not know the ritual; but--there is nothing military about these things nowadays, all is abolished. The soldiers come to change sentinels, talk freely, laugh loudly. Instead of military traditions--like parole, pass-words, exchange of salutes, etc., etc.,--they ask:

"Ah, howdy! What are "they" (meaning the prisoners) doing? Anything to look at? All right--now you go, we'll stay."

They have, however, a tradition. When the changed jailors are assembled near the entrance,--they start to knock on the rain pipes of the Mansion with their rifles, to throw sand and small stones into the windows of the Heir and the Princesses. When they think enough frightening has been done, they start to sing something hideous and pornographic.

"She went to the ma-a-rket,   Bought a bell as a locket...."

begins a thin trembling voice very calmly and even bashfully, as if nothing bad will come out of this quiet song. And then, suddenly, a chorus of twelve big fat swine would belch the notorious refrain:

"Ah, you brunette of mine,   O-oh, curly girl of mine...."

and so forth, with the licentious words of this song accompanying it with whistles and jazzing with bayonettes, field-pans and general noise.

I tried to analyze all of this. Why? Why is there such a hatred for these,--this poor man, these five women and a boy? Such unnecessary torture of people of the past,--nothing but a man who awaits the end of his tragedy, nothing but a frail boy, nothing but five trembling ladies. And the picture of the old woman that broke her hip on the deck--and provoked laughter, comes to me.

The second day of my occupation,--it was about eleven when the sentinels were changed and the night was warm and bluish, the demonstration, perhaps in my honor, was exceptionally noisy and obscene.

"How do you like it?" asked Pashinsky gloriously, looking at me and showing, instead of teeth, a burned-out cemetery in his mouth. "Don't they get enough? They just went to bed--and here is the music."

"Fine!" I answered. "Why don't we shoot? It makes more noise and frightens much more."

"We used to do so," he said with regret, "but all these burjoois, and the popes, and the whole carrion of Tobolsk did not like it. So we have decided for the moment not to. Nobody can forbid singing. We are free. The air belongs to the Soviet Government."

Then he continued:

"You should have seen those little ones"--he winked his eyes--"they got scared to death the first time we sang the "Parson's Daughter" right near their windows! And I'll tell you...." he whispered something in my ear.

I decided to start with him when it comes to rid the world of some of these Reds.

"Good!" I said with extreme pleasure and tapping him on the shoulder, "Where are their rooms?"

"Right where the white curtain hangs ... you see ... one ... two ... three ... fourth window on the second floor. They all are there in one room, they are never alone lately. They used to be on the first floor. That--was a holiday for us boys. Everything seen,--and we would...."

The smile on his face stretched from ear to ear.

"But," he continued,--"again the popes intervened. I hope they'll croak soon. And Kobylinsky consented. He is with us, of course,--but we must get rid of him."

"Well, you boys have good times here," (I said dreamily) "I am glad I came. It's great! All these people had enough of our blood. Now--the people rule themselves! Great life!"

"You bet! Stay with us longer and you'll see better things...."

42

Next day,--it was about four,--Pashinsky, who sticks near me thinking I am his best friend and admirer, punched me with his elbow and said:

"Look, look. Who is coming."

The Emperor, stooping and walking with tottering steps, was passing from the garden into the house. Dr. Botkin was with him. The Emperor's hands were clasped behind him, his eyes were staring downwards. An old, soiled soldier's blouse of khaki flannel was hanging on his spare, bowed, bony body. He was walking slowly, evidently trying to appear indifferent and calm.

I had not seen him for a year and a half or even more. There was more gray in his whiskers,--and to me, at this moment he never seemed to so strikingly resemble his more fortunate English cousin.

They passed very near us. Pashinsky loudly yawned and stretched right in the Emperor's face, who looked at him blankly; but under a dignified and elaborate calm--I detected a spark of wounded majesty. Then he looked at me,--evidently seeing in me nothing but a new jailer,--sighed, and turned his suffering face away. Dr. Botkin looked at me, too; he recognized me with a start.

"Ever see the bloodsucker before? Did you see how I treat him?"

"Never saw him. Where in the hell could I?... As for you--you certainly are some boy!"

I was so near to the Emperor that for a moment I feared he could recognize me. But he did not, for he glanced twice at me and--passed by. When they were on the stairs, Botkin said something to him, and the Emperor turned around, his eyes resting for a moment on my figure. I brought up my hand,--so, that for the Emperor--it was a salute; for Pashinsky--a mosquito which I killed on my forehead. Both Emperor and Botkin immediately turned away and entered the Mansion.

"You watch him closer, Syva," Pashinsky said, "I think we'll take him away for good pretty soon."

Today,--during my watch hours I had time to make observations, especially, when the evening came and the night began.

In the house silent figures were walking; these delicate shadows of yesterday; later--Princess Tatiana sat near the window with a book.

... (line illegible).... has not changed much. From time to time she would stop turning the pages,--and look--without expression, without moving--down at Pashinsky and me, and at the quiet city, at clear skies, at the distant golden crosses shining under the moon.

There was something natural,--and yet not ordinary, in this dark figure behind the curtain.

Did she think of our black ingratitude, she who did so much for the wounded soldiers and for the families of those killed? Did she think of the capricious Fate, which played with her young life so nastily? Did she pray--crushed, humble, and lost? Did she cry for the past, or dream of the future?... Or, perhaps, in her mind was the present,--and behind those noble eyebrows, were thoughts and plans to fight still.... Perhaps there was hope?

This dark figure and the other frightened silhouettes of the endangered ladies in the Mansion, surrounded by their jailers, keep me turning from side to side each night.

I see crooked smiles full of rotting teeth; I see perspiring low foreheads and piercing oily eyes; and I know that New Russia has no compassion.

43

Nachman invited me to a dinner. Later Dutzman came and brought a smirking girl with him. Nothing very interesting. A girl. She sang gypsy songs accompanied by a guitar. Good voice--and bad manners. We had champagne, caviar and cigars,-- real Uppman.

"Eh," he said, "After all--this life is good! Much better even than when I was secretary of the 'Courier of Moscow.' Of course, it is transitory.... Won't you take some more, please?... and we all will be out. Perhaps those of us who will not, by that time, hang, will have already some money put aside. Not I--I am a spender. I can't keep this money."

He was happy and therefore talkative and sincere.

He continued.... "You ask how we get this money? Easily, comrad, very easily, indeed. Besides what we receive from Petrograd, we have other incomes. For instance, here, take this case of the Emperor. Why do you think we intend to send him to Ekaterinburg? Why should we send him towards the approaching Czechs?"

"Everything has been taken by them; they threaten to crush us if the Allies will assist them, even in the slightest way. Still we send. It is a question of two hundred thousand rubles,--but nobody knows that I, Nachman, a scabby Jew, got about fifty thousand out of them. Now another thing: who got the pay for the heavy trucks, and for the benzine, and for the tents, and for the ... oh, many other things!... who got it? This very Nachman, yes, comrad ... have some more, please, it's good!..."

44

"Quod forti placuit legis habet valorem."

Sailor Khokhriakov--the special envoy of the Sovnarkom--and his band. Here is the real danger, but only in case Colonel Kobylinsky and his Detachment of Special Destination would consent to join the Soviets. They all hesitate, not the Colonel, however.

The meeting of the Peoples' Commissaries from Petrograd (Khokhriakov) and Kaganitsky (from Ural, I guess) is certainly worthy of description. I went there, leaving for that reason my Mansion duties--(simply by saying to Pashinsky "tell them I am not coming to the Mansion as I have to attend the meeting"); nowadays military service is really a pleasure.

We all were sitting in the recreation room, about sixty or seventy of us in all. Khokhriakov presided. His neck is like a bull's, but rougher--and red. He started the meeting by a thunderous "Shut up, you over there!" and "Somebody open the window; who in hell is smoking such ... tobacco (I omit the adjective, though correct and strikingly expressive, but profane)?"

The noise stopped under this voice, the windows were thrown open, and our Peoples' Commissary began:

"Comrades,--before us are three questions; 1st--whether to release the prisoners and give them to the Tobolsk people under the auspices of Comrade Kobylinsky and his men, or 2d--whether to try the prisoners right here by the people's tribunal, or 3d--to comply with some other requests--which I have the authority to propose--to send the prisoners to a Ural city. Let us proceed with the first question. I put this proposition to the ballot in this way: the Tobolians, and amongst them the popes, the monarchists, all of the counter-revolutionary trash do not want the Peoples' rule. So they say that the Nikolai family must be given to the Constituent Assembly. Now, what in the hell of hells, do they mean by this? What is a Constituant Assembly? Isn't it a crowd of the same enemies of the people? Isn't this 'Parliament' against our will? Shall we, proletarians, consider the question of a Constituent Assembly? Would it not be an act of counter-revolution? Come out here, right before me, the one that will dare to propose such a thing," and the ten pound wooly fist of the sailor was lifted and held for moments in the filthy air of the recreation room.

This rhetorical question, in fact, was not necessary, as we all, hearing the word "Proletariat" in the middle of Khokhriakov's speech had already started to make a noise and to applaud, the cheers densely hung in the room,--and even before he said, "I knew you are good proletarians and would drown this proposition, God damn you,--carried,"--the fate of this weak and impossible thing at that time, the hope for a Constituent Assembly,--was told. In no way would it do.

"Now comrades,"--Khokhriakov continued after a short confidential chat with the curly, blond, small-faced and long-eared Kaganitsky,--"comes the next proposition. I warn you, however; no matter how tempting this proposition is, do not make any harsh decision. We know your zeal in Petrograd--that's why we all would want you to say your word, but ... if I see that someone is too zealous, I'd rather keep silent if I were he. Can we try these bloodsuckers here?"

An impossible noise began after his words.

"Try?"--"Why? Kill them all, that's all." "Kill the Czar,"--"Kill the brat." "Let them go." "To hell with all of them." "Let's try them, of course." "Give the women to the people." "Put their guts out," etc., etc....

"Shut up you all," shouted Khokhriakov, "let me count the votes. I see you cannot decide, though you all ***don't want the trial*** here! ***Is that so? All right, as you wish, the will of people must prevail. What? Who said it is*** not ***so? Come out you counter-revolutionary, you monarchist, you royal carrion,--come out and say it to*** my face, don't hide, you...." Nobody came out. This categorical imperative could surpass the Kant's.... Kaganitzky's face, smiling, and with moving flappy ears, was in accord with this understanding, and when Khokhriakov barked his--"Carried," he bowed his head.

The audience was then silenced.

"Now, comrades, comes the next proposition,--to send the prisoners away,--to the Ural city, probably Ekaterinburg. Comrade Kaganitzky is here. He says, they will be treated very well (Laughter) and they will not be in danger ***of the Czecks, and popes, and monarchists. The comrades of the detachment and Comrade Kobylinsky--agreed. How do you like*** this? Say, who is against it? Come out!"

Free people in a free country--consented. After which consent a commission under the chairmanship of Kaganitzky was appointed to elaborate particulars. The Detachment of Special Destination was thus dissolved and Comrade Kobylinsky was allowed to proceed to Petrograd.

With a headache from the noise and smoke I left the court-room and went out in the City Square to breathe a little fresh air. Children were playing with sand and toys. Children of the New Russia! Russia of free speech, free thoughts, free ways! God, what will grow out of you?... I wanted to pet one of them, a little thing with gray eyes, but frightened to death of a "Red"--the child yelled and ran; from a distance it shook at me a little trembling fist. So--it is not so bad.

While in the garden--the court room probably was emptied, as few shots were fired behind me,--on the hill, and shortly after, a gala-demonstration started--with a rattling of stones on the roof of the Mansion, whistles, songs and a general delirium of the uncontrolled and wicked mob ...

Feeling the bridles of the High Commissaries, unable to do something to them, understanding the guidance under a sauce of self government, the mob was avenging itself on the inhabitants of the Mansion.

45

I wonder where Lucie is now?

Something heavy and depressing is in my mind this last time; some fog in my thoughts; I think I am losing my standing of a gentleman, dealing with all of these people. My language has become vulgar; my manners, also. I begin....

(few lines scratched out)

46

... This morning Pashinsky repeated that the Em. will be taken to Ekaterinburg with the Empress and the Heir. The daughters will stay here for a while. "Believe me, we'll have a good time," he said, offensively breathing in my face.

I stood near the gates of the fence when Dr. Botkin passed. Nobody was near me, Pashinsky having gone for a drink of water into the quarters. I said without turning my head:

"Decision taken to send only the Em. and Empress and the Heir. Daughters will stay here." Dr. Botkin did not stop. Then, as guard, I did not let him in, and as if I were examining him (that was my right) I said, "Please warn the ladies, and tell the Emperor that the Commissary did not act badly; I guess there is no danger in his going away. I fear for the ladies only."

"You don't mean it! They double-crossed us! They assured us all would go. The scoundrels! Now please let me go,--and thank you, you strange man."

I let him go.

Pashinsky appeared and looked at me. "Are you getting tired of this muzzle, too? Isn't he a ...?"

"Yes," I said, "I must watch him closer now. I think we had better watch him. You stay on the other side, and I'll be here near the windows.

"All right," he said. "Then we can meet here. I'm going to walk from the garden to the fence, and you stay right here. What is your suspicion?"

"Nothing in particular," I answered.... "Just the ordinary one; I don't like him. That's all."

So we walked the way he proposed. Every time he would be near the garden, he would cough in such a noisy and sardonic way that the Heir, who was sitting with Derevenko on the bench would turn his long, pensive face, and his old sailor guardian would look with hatred on the rascal.

When Pashinsky was away, the window behind me opened very cautiously and a lady's voice said to me, "Don't turn. Is it true they are to take Father away? Now, I know you are a gentleman. What would you advise us to do? I think we are all lost."

Pashinsky started to come back; then a Lett passed, so the voice stopped. Pashinsky came near me and said, "The Heir never cries when I tease him. Believe me, he is a hard kid. What do you think if I scare him more?"

"Yes," I said, "a stubborn child." "I must try again," and he walked away.

The window again gave way. "Please," the same voice said, "can't you give any advice to us? We are so frightened! Father is praying; Mother's very ill; we are all alone."

"I'll write you," I said, (without moving my lips), "what I think and bring it back."

"Thank you."

I went to Pashinsky, whose teasing was becoming hideous and rough. He said to the Heir that they had decided to shoot the whole family. Tears were on the child's face but he kept on bravely; he could not go away--Pashinsky was at the gate.

I wished: "Just a day or two,--and I will be able to do something. Oh, God! Send something to stop it right now."

I guess that my prayer was heard.

The tutor's face,--one of those broad Russian faces,--gradually grew purple and then grey. Slowly, and hypnotising Pashinsky, he approached the scamp, took him by the collar and pulled him towards the fence. Then, losing his breath, Derevenko said, "Leave the boy alone, you scoundrel! You,--you call yourself a Russian sailor? You? Have this...." and the slap on Pashinsky's face sounded to me like Chopin's First Nocturne. What divine music!

I expected a clash. But no! The rifle fell out of Pashinsky's hands and, silent and tamed, with half-closed eyes, he was waiting for another smash. Then Derevenko saw me and thought I was going to shoot him, but I made no such move. I slipped away and went innocently towards the big gate. So, when Pashinsky came to me--he was sure I had seen nothing, and when I asked how the teasing was going on, he answered:

"Oh, I let this trash go. It annoys me."

The left side of his face was inflamed and tears were frozen on his eyes. It was a good one, by God!

After this incident I turned to the quarters "for a drink of water" and wrote a little note that "nothing bad could happen to the Princesses when they were alone" and that, "I shall exert all in my power to prevent any disagreeable happenings." I wrote that I knew some people were working to save them. My letter, I thought, would brace them up and would give them an idea that there was, amongst these beasts--one, that would not be an enemy. In case of a struggle this idea would keep them from losing hope and their power of resistance. Then I added that I could be found in the hotel, and that Dr. Botkin knew me.

Contemplating my scratchings, I went over to the window; somebody was patiently waiting and looking around, for the voice said:

"I am so glad Derevenko slapped this awful man."

"I am too, your Highness. Now--there is a letter. I'll put it on the bayonet and stay still; you take it."

Pashinsky passed near me talking with another Red. He felt badly I am sure,--he did not look at me.

I rolled the piece of paper, stuck it on the edge of the sharp bayonet and putting the rifle on my shoulder, directed it towards the window. I felt when it was taken. Then I joined my fellow jailers.

47

Today I saw a man who resembled strikingly the Tumen Russian of the profane language. And it reminded me very much of the Ls., of the English officer, of the fellow with dark eyeglasses--and of Lucie. I felt abandoned again. So I went to the Church, but then turned back: I cannot go in, for it might spoil my reputation of a Red. However, I stood for a bit near the doors and listened to the singers, and then decided to go to the Catholic church, for only Russian Reds must not pray; Polish Reds happen to have this privilege.

There is no difference in fact. I wanted to be closer to something elevated.

The lights were so quiet and peaceful looking in the dark church through high-colored windows. There were not many people in their church, so I could concentrate. But instead of a Christian quiet, I got something else. I guess the idea came to me when I thought that Pashinsky was a Pole.

I began to think that I could not do very much here,--but still something. They will try to annoy the Princesses, and I must protect them. Thus--my staying here will be justified. If Pashinsky or the Letts should do something that would be bad, I'll kill them,--or some of them. When I thought of it, I looked at the Holy Faces; the sun came out of the white clouds, the rays fell on the walls,--and the Faces smiled at me. "Yes," I thought, "if my decision is not agreeable,--the sun will hide behind the clouds again. I'll wait for five minutes"--the sun did not hide,--so--this was accepted. Then I tried to figure how to do it, and found a way. I'll get Pashinsky at the first attempt.

My God, what nonsense I think of!...

48

Schtolz. Jackson. Vieren. The man with the wounded leg. Kitser. Dutzman. Khokhriakov. Fost. Pashinsky. Kart. Fedor. Laksman. Vassiliev (son). Kobylinsky. Perkel. Niestadt. Cymes. Leibner. Vert. Wang-Lee. Frenkel. The fat Kister. Vygardt....

(a few lines scratched out)

49

The "Kitai" was at the pier when we--the detachment of twelve, guarding a silent man and a hysterical woman--came there under the cover of night; it was raining, though the air was warm. The Irtysh stood fragrant with this odor of a big, noble river. The waters--in which sank Yermak under his heavy corselet--the same waters were carrying toward the unknown--the Imperial Family.

Though their departure was supposed to be made in secrecy, there was a crowd of people on the pier--we tried to chase them away, but they stood there. An ascetic figure was standing on the next pier, lit only by a few lanterns. This black figure lifted a cross and blessed the Emperor, who tenderly released his hand from the spasmatic grip of his terrified wife and made the sign of the cross.

"Quit that, Reverend scoundrel," I heard Khokhriakov's voice. "Who asked you to come?"

The priest answered:

"Thou knowest not what thou art committing."

"Ah, shut up! To hell with your citations, you old idiot!"

"Take him down over there. Isn't there anyone to choke him?" continued Khokhriakov bending over the hand-rails. "This ass is propagating,--don't you see, comrades?"

No one, however, moved. This crowd around the Bishop all answered. Their answer,--a blunt roaring,--sounded like distant thunder and there was such a frightening unity in this dull noise,--that I had the shivers.

"You cowards!" bellowed the sailor, "I'll have to come back and finish with the pope myself! It will not be the first one, anyhow. It's too late now! Be damned you all! Go ahead!" The gangplanks dropped.

The steamer started to move.

The priest stood still blessing her passengers,--the Emperor, the Empress, the bolsheviki,--the crew,--all, all of them. And, wet under the rain, this figure vested in black, with a shiny cross lifted high in the air, will for a long time remain in my memory.

The Mansion was black; not a light in the windows. The four girls, left alone in this nest of rattlesnakes,--were probably sitting in some far distant corner,--crying, trembling, praying,--and waiting for the worst, which they feared was coming.

50

To kill a man? Nothing more agreeable if it is the right one,--I should say! And in such country where the trial is impossible. I did not know I ever could,--but...

Pashinsky started soon after the Emperor was taken. He and Fost asked me for a conference behind the quarters, when we were waiting to change the watchmen. Both had a confidential expression on their faces.

"You see here, Syva,--what is planned. You and Fost stay under the windows, and go around, just as you please. I'll go upstairs, and listen. If there is no one around I'll call you up. I know that they are all alone."

I consented, and when they left I wrote a note: "Si, se soir, quelcun tache de forcer l'entree de votre chambre, je vous implore de rester calme et sure que je suis avec Vous et Vos soeurs a vous proteger. Ne craignez rien, ne criez pas!" I wrote it in French in order to assure them of the faith in me--and prove my identity--and signed my real name.

It looked funny to me; I think now I am Syvorotka,--honestly Syvorotka, formerly of the 7th of Hussars!

I went out and looked around. The Pole and the Lett were talking and gazing from time to time at the upper windows. Then the Pole approached: "How much would you take from me not to go up at all, and let me do it alone?" and then, becoming sweet and fawning--.

"You see, Syva," he said, "Fost consented. Why shouldn't you? I'll give you just as much."

"Did you consent, Fost?" I asked.

"Yes," said the Lett, digging in his short nose, "I did. I have grown-up daughters at home. I cannot. Besides he gives me money, so why shouldn't I? I will stay in the corridor and won't let anybody come in, on this side of the House. I know nothing of your business. Go on, have your pleasure."

"No, Pashinsky," I said, "that will not do. I must be with you. I have to protect you besides, you idiot; Fost can only see what is in the house, but supposing someone comes from down here? You think they will forget such an outrage to the Soviets? I will be with you somewhere behind, and when you call me I will come out. Hope you won't forget me."

Pashinsky thought over my proposition for a second,--thinking was a strenuous effort for him. His obscene face wore a suffering and preoccupied expression; then he said:

"I think you are right. We'll let Fost stay and watch the inner doors, and you and I will be alone in this side of the house. Then the men on the streets can't catch us, and we will be protected from the inside too...."

Then he had some idea. A bad one, I am sure!

"All right, that's a good way, anyhow. Now I am going to take a bath,--I need it. If somebody asks for me, say so."

The Lett and I remained. I stood for half an hour near my window,--then it opened. I fixed the note on the bayonette and it went to its destination.

After, a voice said:

"Mister * * *, we are afraid! What can we do? Do you think that you can protect us? Please tell the truth, don't try to console us."

"I am sure, your Highness," I said, "please don't worry."

The voice continued: "They took out the keys from the doors. We cannot even lock ourselves in, or hide. Can't you tell this to the Budishchev's--perhaps they can do something?"

"You shouldn't try to hide, and there is no use to tell it to anybody, believe me. Be in the room on the second floor and wait there. I will be on the watch as I said."

--"You know better perhaps,--we believe you."

With a "Thank you so much" and "We are so frightened!" repeated with despair and horror, the window closed.

I had to invent something, and invent quickly, for I had no plan as yet.

The Browning was with me but I reserved it for the last chance, and I decided to keep it loaded to finish some of the Reds--and myself--if it should come to an open fight. With such thoughts I was desperately rambling within the fence.

My vague plan was to come right after Pashinsky and knock him on the head with something heavy,--then I rejected this project: the scoundrel could yell and I would be discovered. I came to the quarters and looked around. It was the office of Tanaevsky before occupied by us. In the classic disorder, with an inch of cigarette butts and dust on the floor, among the remnants of the Governor's House stored here, I saw a gold metallic rope cord which in better times had been used to support the heavy drapery of the reception room. The idea of a silent strangulation came into my head with the picture of Jacolliot's Thugs. I cut the tassel away and put it under somebody's pillow, and hid the rope in my bosom.

At seven Pashinsky finally came back, surprisingly clean, shaven, and smelling of some cheap and penetrating perfume. He was slightly drunk. When clean,--he looked to me a thousand times worse.

Neither Pashinsky, nor I, could wait until the night came. He was continually repeating what I should do, and continually asking me whether I thought everything was safe. Finally night arrived. At nine the lights in the Mansion were put out--all but in one window. I knew how hearts were beating there: mine was echoing.

--"I am going, Syva," Pashinsky whispered. "I can't wait any longer--all is burning inside of me."

He put his rifle behind the rain-pipe, straightened his belt, and started towards the entrance door.

The door of the Mansion squeaked and swallowed him, and before I heard him walking up the stairs I followed him.

All was dark inside, only a feeble light from the court penetrated through the windows. We passed the corridor, then a large room, then a small room. Here Pashinsky stopped--and I heard his heavy breathing. Then he threw open the door.

I saw mattresses on the floor and in a far corner pale, trembling figures, glued together by fear.

Pashinsky hesitated for a moment--to pick out the one he wanted--and then with an outcry, suddenly rushed to this mass of helpless panic-stricken bodies, and a struggle between a delirious man, feebled by desire, and these ladies, began.

I jumped on him from behind; preoccupied, he did not feel when I put the rope around his neck so that the collar wouldn't be in my way, tightened my weapon in a deadlock and dragged him away--almost before his carnal touch contaminated the Princesses--into the next room, and shut the doors.

He was making some efforts to free himself, hitting my knees with his heels, and growling from rage; then he bit me in the hand. But in a minute I was already firmly sitting on his back, with my knees on his awkwardly turned arms, twisting the rope with all of the strength I had.

"Please, don't kill him," I heard a sobbing whispering voice say, and other voices, too, repeated the "don't kill."

This Kerensky idea made me quite angry and I said as calmly as I could under the circumstances:

"With all of my reverence for your order, your Highnesses, I refuse to obey. Please shut the doors and don't wake up the others,--I have my own accounts to settle." And when the doors closed, I kept tightening and tightening the rope until his head turned and his tongue,--rough and dry,--came way out and was touching my hands, and his face became hot and wet. He made a few convulsive movements--and became still.

When his head fell with a dull sound on the floor, I took him out under cover of the night, and threw his body into the well. I walked out onto Tuliatskaya Street and chatted for a while with Leibner and Vert.

I was changed and nobody asked me where my friend Pashinsky was.

51

Comrade Fost was shot yesterday at nine in the morning for murder. It was a glorious inspiration to put the tassel under his pillow. In the afternoon we buried Pashinsky. I gave my share for a wreath with red ribbons and the inscription "To him who fell for Proletariat--Long live the International," and was present at the funeral. Dutzman made a speech; a very pathetic one.

In the evening the sentinels were doubled. There are lights in every room now. There was a light in every corridor. The ladies--are,--for the moment being, out of immediate danger. The Soviet decided to transport all to Ekaterinburg,--as soon as a steamer will be available.

Today Nachman called on me. He took me to the Square and when we were sitting on a bench, he said, that "It was well done" ("that's all right, sir, perfectly all right"), but if he were in my place he would go away. "It's easy," he continued,--"supposing I give you a good letter of recommendation to my people in Ekaterinburg? The interesting part of all of this,--believe me, has started only. Don't fear me,--this scabby Jew, this very Nachman,--will not betray."

I thought it over and said:

"I would do so, if I only could leave some trace here. A friend may ask for me here, and I would be sore if she could not find me,--if she only cares."

"Oh, she will," he laughed, "she will. Of course, I am not posted in your personal affairs, but--a lady always can find *one,* if she cares. Ha-ha-ha! Youth is always youth! But you better go without leaving traces...."

I continued:

"Nachman, there is another thing. Here is an old man,--a friend of mine,--he is very sick. His days are numbered, and I feel very sorry for him. If I go away all will be lost for this old chap; he has nobody in this world. Could you use your power and place him in a hospital? I will give you money, of course,--I have some."

Nachman sighed: "This is so out of time! Nowadays love and charity are much more dangerous than murders and thefts."

Then after a pause, he continued;

"Very well, friend, I will take care of your man. Hand me the money."

Then he gave me a letter to his friends in Ekaterinburg (it was ready in his pocket) and we parted.

I am free, happy, independent, with a good standing amongst the present Russians. And if only she could be near me ... but there is no perfect happiness on this strangest of planets of ours.

52

(pages missing)

... heavy trucks, and other military paraphernalia. Some of the men on them surely are not Russians, Letts, or Germans, or ...

(nine lines scratched out)

... I don't know whether it was Nachman's talk or the truth.

Anyhow I am going away,--again alone,--alone forever. Damn life! I cannot look backwards--I feel sorry for my past; the present--is sufficiently bad not to speak of it; the future--is just as dark--as this night. Not a star, not a single star.

The old man was taken to the People's Hospital this afternoon. He thanked me.

53

... starting rumors of the killing of the whole Family, and always emphasizing that this tragedy--was the supreme penalty brought to the altar by the Emperor.

Nachman, and others, who--it seems to me, know what they are talking about, foresee many chances; the best of them, is of course the fact, that some ...

(few lines scratched out)

... are in this enterprise, and therefore it might be crowned with success. I really do not know what to think. Only one point is clear: I cannot believe that our sufferings, the sufferings of the whole country, are unknown beyond our frontiers. They must be known; the tears shed cannot during so long a time fall on stones,--even stones get wet. If they are not known,--these sufferings,--if our hands stretched for help are not seen, if we are condemned just for the only fact that we are Russians,--and if ...

(a page missing)

54

... knocked at the door. I hardly had time to say "enter," when something enveloped in a thick brown overcoat rolled in, jumped at me and in a second covered all of my face with hot kisses. I answered them very attentively.

Then I noticed that the amiable creature was Lucie.

"No, you don't hate me! No, you don't hate me! I know it! I knew it!..."

"Lucie," I said, "before we proceed, please let me put some of these papers in my pockets."

"Alex! Don't remind me of that! How did you dare to write such stories about me? You can't blame me, can you?"

"Perhaps I don't--for some pages you destroyed. How about the chart, and about the?..."

She covered my mouth with her hands. "If we recollect everything it will be endless. And besides I don't think I took anything from you. Let's forget! I'll forgive you, if you promise me not to write nasty stories about your Lucie."

I promised, and consented, of course. How can I do otherwise? No use!

I put her near me, poured her some tea and offered her the cookies.

For a time we looked at each other. She certainly looked like a peasant girl!

"How do you like this costume?" she said. "Next bal masque I certainly will wear this kind, you may be sure. Of course all of this, and that must be chiffon, and silk, and...." A woman cannot get on without these chats. On the other hand--woman speaks to the man about it with a concealed contempt: what does a man **understand? She does not get angry when she sees that the man does not listen; he only** looks.

"Now,"--she said, gazing around with a dear grimace,--"again in your element, in dirt? What shall I do with you, Alex? I can't stand it!"

"Dirt is my protection, dear. Why did you leave? Don't run away any more."

"We will see about it. But first--what are you doing here? Are you following me? Don't you think I saw you here? Why do you risk your life? How did you think of leaving Tumen? How is your cook?"

"Do your *questions give* me the same right of investigation? I'll answer you, anyhow. I've decided to lay down my cards, Lucie. I came here on business. I broke all ties. Nobody wants me. I am investigating at my own expense, at my own risk, out of curiosity only. But I am free. Don't you need me? Don't you need a friend? Can't we live without deceiving each other, without robbing,--eh? I came here, Lucie,--and behind all of my intentions was one thing only: I hoped to find you, and tell you how much I love you. I knew you had to be near the center, and the center is, at least now--here. Don't lie to me, bad girl, I know what I am talking about. Now--when I think we again will part--I have chills; especially when I think of your manner of going away: pinning a "good-by" to the cushion. Please, let us be together!"

"You should not tempt me, Alex. I feel just as you do, only--I don't think I can even dream of our being together--right now, I mean. What will be after--we'll see."

"Cannot you arrange something for me so that I could be with you in your business? Did not you ask me before to do so? Now--I come to you."

"It's true, I did. Things have changed. Can you believe me when I swear I am telling the truth? Yes? You'll try? Well, I wanted you in Petrograd--you fascinated me; that was all,--and if then, after being with us, you had come to know too much and something had happened to you, I would, of course, have been sorry,--but,-- how shall I say it? Not too much. In Tumen,--you know I came to Syvorotka with certain purposes: you described them well in your diary, so well that I had to put my censorship on them,--I did not suspect Syvorotka was--you...."

I made an impatient movement. "Again your fairy tale?"

"Alex!" she exclaimed, "I conjure you to believe me! Can't you see? Get me to tell you the truth when I am so happy as now! I could not lie to you! So that's how I came to Tumen. You were there, and you know what happened. Now--don't laugh at me,--I understand that you risked too much,--and I ran away, because I saw--I loved you. I'd die if I knew something had happened to you on account of me. I told them that you had gone to Kazan, or Nijni, that you had turned into a real bolshevik. They think you are out. For them--you are lost. And they must not see you here."

"Who are 'they'? And how about you knowing too much?" I inquired. "Your mysteries don't sound grave anyhow."

"Alex,--I'll be angry! Again you ask silly things."

So I kissed her and asked how Stanley was and the Russian and the Letts, and the pony.

"Poor little thing! It died. We tried to reach Tobolsk with it."

"Your Stanley poisoned it with his chimney," I said.

"Don't hold anything against him, Alex. He is a good fellow. And don't be jealous, you bad, dirty, lovable crank. He still thinks you are a Canadian."

"He never thinks. He fancies."

She laughed. "Yes, you are jealous. It is silly of you, but agreeable. I did not know you could be."

"Now, let's be serious. You can't stay here. I must insist on your going away,--dear, for your own sake,--for our sake! I promise it won't be for a long time,--perhaps it will only seem so, if you love me! Don't say no. Can't you picture how happy we can be afterwards? How somewhere away from here we could marry, and.... You must go away. Why not go to England, or Japan, or Sweden? Just a trip?"

"How funny you talk!" I said. "Listen to my reasons. One: I must stay near you. Two: I must see the end of this tragedy. Three: I must close my bit of an account with some people. Four: All I have is not enough to pay for this room,--so no trips for me. Five: ..."

"Stop! Stop!" she exclaimed, and crawling into my lap, continued:

"My poor boy! That--is killing! I know why you are so poor! You spent every penny on others! You had some earnings! And to think of all you were bringing to me in Tumen ... then you did not care even, but just to be hospitable to an intruder.... And other things.... How can I repay you!..."

"There are no reasons for crying on this account. Forget it please. Don't put me in the light of a benefactor,--I hate it."

"No, no! I feel so guilty now. I'll give you money."

"Don't offend me. All I want is not to be an idiot in the future and not to lose you. So I have said it,--and it is said. When it comes to stubbornness--I hardly think anybody could beat me. So just understand: I am going to stay ***where you are, and if you try this time to get away, I'll have to take measures. I'll kidnap you. I'll put you in a place where no 'Navy-Cut' is smoked. Now--it*** is serious. Understand?"

We talked, and argued, and even quarrelled, and again made peace, until she declared herself beaten. Maybe she was angry; perhaps scared; but surely greatly flattered. A woman is a woman--always flattered when she sees persistence. She consented to take me into her game. I had to swear, and cross my heart, and give endless words of honor,--all that for a position of a traffic man, like the one in Tumen. I had to swear that no cooks, or maids, or ladies (especially ladies!) would distract me from the thought of her. Very selfish, but understandable. It was late, when she left me.

"Alex," she said on the threshold,--"Please don't talk. Do not write, please! You'll have time to finish your diary, and write even a series of books on the subject afterwards. Maybe I'll help you even. Close your diary. Give it to me, I'll hide it!..."

"Is that ***so?" I said,--"there is nothing now that would be of interest*** to you."

"Everything interests me, dear. Aren't you mean to your Lucie?... Very well, hide it yourself, burn it, if you can't hide it. Can't you keep in your mind your impressions? Do you promise? Consider me too!"

"I promise. I'll do it. I must only write all about this evening. Every word. This evening I almost trust you. It is of historical value therefore."

She gave her consent.

When the door closed after her, and my lips were still burning, hideous phantoms of doubt poured into the room; they tortured me, and sneered at me, and kept me awake....

And with the pale rose of the first sunrays the phantoms of doubt left me exhausted, miserable and helpless like a wet cat.

*　　*　　*　　*　　*

Translator's note.

With paragraph **55** ends the diary of Syvorotka.

Among his documents, however, has been found the following letter, not in his characteristic handwriting, but in that of someone else, bearing directly upon the incidents narrated by the diarist. Written in ungrammatical Russian, bearing many orthographic mistakes, this document seems to be a fragment of a report, by some unidentified co-operating agent, to his unrevealed superior.

It is deemed necessary, therefore, for purposes of clearness, to append this document, as I find it among the literary remains of Al. Syvorotka:

55

... "four or five days after your departure, I gave the story to P.D.; he took it to the E * * * *; the latter made but a few corrections in it, and P.D. copied it,--as you ordered: with different ink, and on different paper. The fourteenth passed quietly. The new man who took command of the guards and his assistant, assembled the men and organized a meeting; Syvorotka was present. Some of the people spoke of the "hidden treasury"; some spoke of the People's Tribunal; some insisted upon a wholesale killing,--for the loyals and the Czechs are rapidly approaching, and from everywhere come rumors about uprisings. Finally it was decided to try the Family immediately.

The next day we were busy with the trucks; towards evening all of them were in shape including the Number 74-M in which you ordered the change of magneto, and ready to move. So you see-- we have done what you ordered, and if all happened so that we could not foresee, it was not my fault, nor Syvorotka's, nor Phillip's.

All the day of the 16th the investigation continued, and the Commissaries asked for the E * * * * twice; once four men went to Ipatiev's; their conduct was outrageous. At eight in the evening I was on my post in the red house, the wires were working fine and Philip answered. Nachman's place answered too.

At nine I signalled to the Ipatiev's, and Princess waved "all well," but could not continue for a Red came to the window and shut it with a bayonet. It had already begun to get very dark, so I phoned again to Philip and Syvorotka and asked them whether they had orders to start. I was told that they had not heard anything from the house. I decided to wait a little longer and then to 'phone to Tikhvinsky to inquire whether or not the Nun was on her place, so I could go and investigate why

S-y did not start. At ten I called up, but the 'phone was dead. While I was waiting for some movement about the house, Philip himself came and said that S-y had ordered him to remove the trucks away out of the city. Philip refused to do so, and tried to reach me by 'phone but it was out of order, so he left Syvorotka in charge and came to ask me personally. While we were trying to digest what all of this meant and what should be done, a movement began in the house; lights flickered in the windows and shortly afterwards, we distinctly heard the report of a revolver. As this looked bad we both left and ran across the place, but the Reds would not let anybody in. Already there were about fifteen men trying to break down the fence. The inside guards resisted and some shots were exchanged. The assailants were Reds, asking for "a treasury," and some of them were asking for the Family as it was rumored that they had already been killed.

Seeing that nothing could be done from this side I went to the rear and squeezed in, for Ch. was there and he let me do so; but he said that he had heard shots inside and that he thought all was finished, and said also that Leinst and three others went to search in Syvorotka's home--they evidently don't know that all was taken out yesterday. In the house I found complete commotion. The family had disappeared, and no one knew where or how. Pytkan was shot in the stomach and in the throat and I saw him lying on the floor in the room. Khokhriakov and his men were shaking the rest of his life out of him, asking where the E. and the jewelry were, but all that Pytkan could say was "they were taken away." No one could make out what really had happened and who had shot him; some said that they went away in trucks, yet, in the evening, some that a detachment sent by the Soviet took them secretly out, some said aeroplanes. All were wrong, for Philip had just come back and the trucks were in place, no one came into the Ipatiev's house as I was on guard, and there had been no aeroplanes since six o'clock. Pytkan was almost dead when Khokhriakov finally got from him that the family had been shot and taken away-- and then he began to expire. Later the German appeared and chased us all away,-- he sent for his assistant, but they could not find him.

The family disappeared,--it is true; there was no trace of them. I continued to look everywhere up to the time that the Soviet representatives arrived, having been ordered to arrest all people who were with the family, and commenced searching for the bodies. The whole place was surrounded by Reds, and all were ordered out, but nothing was there. Then a resolution was made that the prisoners had been taken away and shot, and they sent a wire to Moscow. I only know that inside the house they killed two people and nobody else, anyhow. Pytkan and Kramer were dead; Kramer probably had been shot from a distance--the bullet was in his head. There were no more than two men killed, I know it; so you may feel sure, when you hear that all were killed in the house that it is a lie. Somebody must have been burning things in the stove long before--maybe in the daytime or the early evening; the stove was almost cold,--the Reds got something out of it, I did not see what it was. When I understood that the whole family had been taken away, dead or alive, or had somehow disappeared, and that there was nothing for us to do, I took Philip and we rushed back to Syvorotka. The trucks and the chauffeurs were all gone. In the garage we found Syvorotka tied with a rope and shot in the spine, and bleeding from scratches and other wounds. From the appearance of the garage we understood that there had been a struggle, but he could not speak comprehensively; all we got from him were moanings, separate phrases and words like "treason," "run away," "leave me die here," etc., etc.,--he was decidedly raving and very weak. We helped him as best we could and came back to the city at about five in the morning and Philip went to Nachman's. They both reported that shortly after two o'clock, three of the trucks passed on the highway to Sysertsky Works. Some people were in them, and the Nachmans thought it was our affair, for the rumors had already reached them that the family had disappeared or had been executed. This Sysertsky direction is more or less correct for I know from Syvorotka that supplies were lately being sent continuously with him to Tubiuk. This way also went Syvorotka's woman.

S-y and all the rest left,--some people say in the evening, some early in the morning of the 17th.

Maybe something could be told by Syvorotka if he ever survives his wounds, and if the Reds do not find him and finish him before they leave, for he is under suspicion. He still is unconscious, and has fever. All Philip and I know is that either all our organization has failed to succeed, or we were all betrayed and sold, or that you intentionally detracted our attention from the truth.

This letter will be given to you by Mrs. Nachman who is going tonight to Ufa. As soon as the Reds leave Ekaterinburg we will both follow,--we are hiding now,-- and will report on the facts that we witnessed and the rumors we heard."

The Codes Of Hammurabi And Moses
W. W. Davies

QTY

The discovery of the Hammurabi Code is one of the greatest achievements of archaeology, and is of paramount interest, not only to the student of the Bible, but also to all those interested in ancient history...

Religion   **ISBN:** *1-59462-338-4*

Pages:132

MSRP $12.95

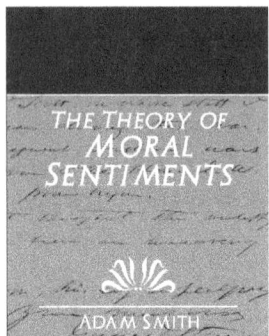

The Theory of Moral Sentiments
Adam Smith

QTY

This work from 1749. contains original theories of conscience amd moral judgment and it is the foundation for systemof morals.

Philosophy **ISBN:** *1-59462-777-0*

Pages:536

MSRP $19.95

Jessica's First Prayer
Hesba Stretton

QTY

In a screened and secluded corner of one of the many railway-bridges which span the streets of London there could be seen a few years ago, from five o'clock every morning until half past eight, a tidily set-out coffee-stall, consisting of a trestle and board, upon which stood two large tin cans, with a small fire of charcoal burning under each so as to keep the coffee boiling during the early hours of the morning when the work-people were thronging into the city on their way to their daily toil...

Childrens   **ISBN:** *1-59462-373-2*

Pages:84

MSRP $9.95

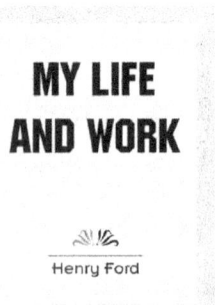

My Life and Work
Henry Ford

QTY

Henry Ford revolutionized the world with his implementation of mass production for the Model T automobile. Gain valuable business insight into his life and work with his own auto-biography... "We have only started on our development of our country we have not as yet, with all our talk of wonderful progress, done more than scratch the surface. The progress has been wonderful enough but..."

Biographies/   **ISBN:** *1-59462-198-5*

Pages:300

MSRP $21.95

The Art of Cross-Examination
Francis Wellman

QTY

I presume it is the experience of every author, after his first book is published upon an important subject, to be almost overwhelmed with a wealth of ideas and illustrations which could readily have been included in his book, and which to his own mind, at least, seem to make a second edition inevitable. Such certainly was the case with me; and when the first edition had reached its sixth impression in five months, I rejoiced to learn that it seemed to my publishers that the book had met with a sufficiently favorable reception to justify a second and considerably enlarged edition. ..

Pages:412

Reference   ISBN: *1-59462-647-2*   *MSRP $19.95*

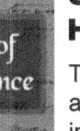

On the Duty of Civil Disobedience
Henry David Thoreau

QTY

Thoreau wrote his famous essay, On the Duty of Civil Disobedience, as a protest against an unjust but popular war and the immoral but popular institution of slave-owning. He did more than write—he declined to pay his taxes, and was hauled off to gaol in consequence. Who can say how much this refusal of his hastened the end of the war and of slavery ?

Law   ISBN: *1-59462-747-9*   **Pages:48**

MSRP $7.45

Dream Psychology Psychoanalysis for Beginners
Sigmund Freud

QTY

Sigmund Freud, born Sigismund Schlomo Freud (May 6, 1856 - September 23, 1939), was a Jewish-Austrian neurologist and psychiatrist who co-founded the psychoanalytic school of psychology. Freud is best known for his theories of the unconscious mind, especially involving the mechanism of repression; his redefinition of sexual desire as mobile and directed towards a wide variety of objects; and his therapeutic techniques, especially his understanding of transference in the therapeutic relationship and the presumed value of dreams as sources of insight into unconscious desires.

Pages:196

Dream Psychology
Psychoanalysis for Beginners

Sigmund Freud

Psychology   ISBN: *1-59462-905-6*   *MSRP $15.45*

The Miracle of Right Thought
Orison Swett Marden

QTY

Believe with all of your heart that you will do what you were made to do. When the mind has once formed the habit of holding cheerful, happy, prosperous pictures, it will not be easy to form the opposite habit. It does not matter how improbable or how far away this realization may see, or how dark the prospects may be, if we visualize them as best we can, as vividly as possible, hold tenaciously to them and vigorously struggle to attain them, they will gradually become actualized, realized in the life. But a desire, a longing without endeavor, a yearning abandoned or held indifferently will vanish without realization.

Pages:360

Self Help   ISBN: *1-59462-644-8*   *MSRP $25.45*

www.bookjungle.com *email: sales@bookjungle.com fax: 630-214-0564 mail: Book Jungle PO Box 2226 Champaign, IL 61825*

QTY

The Rosicrucian Cosmo-Conception Mystic Christianity *by Max Heindel*   ISBN: *1-59462-188-8*   **$38.95**
The Rosicrucian Cosmo-conception is not dogmatic, neither does it appeal to any other authority than the reason of the student. It is: not controversial, but is: sent forth in the, hope that it may help to clear...   New Age/Religion Pages 646

Abandonment To Divine Providence *by Jean-Pierre de Caussade*   ISBN: *1-59462-228-0*   **$25.95**
"The Rev. Jean Pierre de Caussade was one of the most remarkable spiritual writers of the Society of Jesus in France in the 18th Century. His death took place at Toulouse in 1751. His works have gone through many editions and have been republished...   Inspirational/Religion Pages 400

Mental Chemistry *by Charles Haanel*   ISBN: *1-59462-192-6*   **$23.95**
Mental Chemistry allows the change of material conditions by combining and appropriately utilizing the power of the mind. Much like applied chemistry creates something new and unique out of careful combinations of chemicals the mastery of mental chemistry...   New Age Pages 354

The Letters of Robert Browning and Elizabeth Barret Barrett 1845-1846 vol II   ISBN: *1-59462-193-4*   **$35.95**
by Robert Browning and Elizabeth Barrett   Biographies Pages 596

Gleanings In Genesis (volume I) *by Arthur W. Pink*   ISBN: *1-59462-130-6*   **$27.45**
Appropriately has Genesis been termed "the seed plot of the Bible" for in it we have, in germ form, almost all of the great doctrines which are afterwards fully developed in the books of Scripture which follow...   Religion/Inspirational Pages 420

The Master Key *by L. W. de Laurence*   ISBN: *1-59462-001-6*   **$30.95**
In no branch of human knowledge has there been a more lively increase of the spirit of research during the past few years than in the study of Psychology, Concentration and Mental Discipline. The requests for authentic lessons in Thought Control, Mental Discipline and...   New Age/Business Pages 422

The Lesser Key Of Solomon Goetia *by L. W. de Laurence*   ISBN: *1-59462-092-X*   **$9.95**
This translation of the first book of the "Lemegton" which is now for the first time made accessible to students of Talismanic Magic was done, after careful collation and edition, from numerous Ancient Manuscripts in Hebrew, Latin, and French...   New Age/Occult Pages 92

Rubaiyat Of Omar Khayyam *by Edward Fitzgerald*   ISBN:*1-59462-332-5*   **$13.95**
Edward Fitzgerald, whom the world has already learned, in spite of his own efforts to remain within the shadow of anonymity, to look upon as one of the rarest poets of the century, was born at Bredfield, in Suffolk, on the 31st of March, 1809. He was the third son of John Purcell...   Music Pages 172

Ancient Law *by Henry Maine*   ISBN: *1-59462-128-4*   **$29.95**
The chief object of the following pages is to indicate some of the earliest ideas of mankind, as they are reflected in Ancient Law, and to point out the relation of those ideas to modern thought.   Religion/History Pages 452

Far-Away Stories *by William J. Locke*   ISBN: *1-59462-129-2*   **$19.45**
"Good wine needs no bush, but a collection of mixed vintages does. And this book is just such a collection. Some of the stories I do not want to remain buried for ever in the museum files of dead magazine-numbers an author's not unpardonable vanity..."   Fiction Pages 272

Life of David Crockett *by David Crockett*   ISBN: *1-59462-250-7*   **$27.45**
"Colonel David Crockett was one of the most remarkable men of the times in which he lived. Born in humble life, but gifted with a strong will, an indomitable courage, and unremitting perseverance...   Biographies/New Age Pages 424

Lip-Reading *by Edward Nitchie*   ISBN: *1-59462-206-X*   **$25.95**
Edward B. Nitchie, founder of the New York School for the Hard of Hearing, now the Nitchie School of Lip-Reading, Inc, wrote "LIP-READING Principles and Practice". The development and perfecting of this meritorious work on lip-reading was an undertaking...   How-to Pages 400

A Handbook of Suggestive Therapeutics, Applied Hypnotism, Psychic Science   ISBN: *1-59462-214-0*   **$24.95**
by Henry Munro   Health/New Age/Health/Self-help Pages 376

A Doll's House: and Two Other Plays *by Henrik Ibsen*   ISBN: *1-59462-112-8*   **$19.95**
Henrik Ibsen created this classic when in revolutionary 1848 Rome. Introducing some striking concepts in playwriting for the realist genre, this play has been studied the world over.   Fiction/Classics/Plays 308

The Light of Asia *by sir Edwin Arnold*   ISBN: *1-59462-204-3*   **$13.95**
In this poetic masterpiece, Edwin Arnold describes the life and teachings of Buddha. The man who was to become known as Buddha to the world was born as Prince Gautama of India but he rejected the worldly riches and abandoned the reigns of power when...   Religion/History/Biographies Pages 170

The Complete Works of Guy de Maupassant *by Guy de Maupassant*   ISBN: *1-59462-157-8*   **$16.95**
"For days and days, nights and nights, I had dreamed of that first kiss which was to consecrate our engagement, and I knew not on what spot I should put my lips..."   Fiction/Classics Pages 240

The Art of Cross-Examination *by Francis L. Wellman*   ISBN: *1-59462-309-0*   **$26.95**
Written by a renowned trial lawyer, Wellman imparts his experience and uses case studies to explain how to use psychology to extract desired information through questioning.   How-to/Science/Reference Pages 408

Answered or Unanswered? *by Louisa Vaughan*   ISBN: *1-59462-248-5*   **$10.95**
Miracles of Faith in China   Religion Pages 112

The Edinburgh Lectures on Mental Science (1909) *by Thomas*   ISBN: *1-59462-008-3*   **$11.95**
This book contains the substance of a course of lectures recently given by the writer in the Queen Street Hail, Edinburgh. Its purpose is to indicate the Natural Principles governing the relation between Mental Action and Material Conditions...   New Age/Psychology Pages 148

Ayesha *by H. Rider Haggard*   ISBN: *1-59462-301-5*   **$24.95**
Verily and indeed it is the unexpected that happens! Probably if there was one person upon the earth from whom the Editor of this, and of a certain previous history, did not expect to hear again...   Classics Pages 380

Ayala's Angel *by Anthony Trollope*   ISBN: *1-59462-352-X*   **$29.95**
The two girls were both pretty, but Lucy who was twenty-one who supposed to be simple and comparatively unattractive, whereas Ayala was credited, as her Bombwhat romantic name might show, with poetic charm and a taste for romance. Ayala when her father died was nineteen...   Fiction Pages 484

The American Commonwealth *by James Bryce*   ISBN: *1-59462-286-8*   **$34.45**
An interpretation of American democratic political theory. It examines political mechanics and society from the perspective of Scotsman James Bryce   Politics Pages 572

Stories of the Pilgrims *by Margaret P. Pumphrey*   ISBN: *1-59462-116-0*   **$17.95**
This book explores pilgrims religious oppression in England as well as their escape to Holland and eventual crossing to America on the Mayflower, and their early days in New England...   History Pages 268

QTY

The Fasting Cure *by Sinclair Upton*   ISBN: *1-59462-222-1*   **$13.95**

In the Cosmopolitan Magazine for May, 1910, and in the Contemporary Review (London) for April, 1910, I published an article dealing with my experiences in fasting. I have written a great many magazine articles, but never one which attracted so much attention... New Age/Self Help/Health Pages 164

☐

Hebrew Astrology *by Sepharial*   ISBN: *1-59462-308-2*   **$13.45**

In these days of advanced thinking it is a matter of common observation that we have left many of the old landmarks behind and that we are now pressing forward to greater heights and to a wider horizon than that which represented the mind-content of our progenitors...   Astrology Pages 144

☐

Thought Vibration or The Law of Attraction in the Thought World   ISBN: *1-59462-127-6*   **$12.95**

by William Walker Atkinson   *Psychology/Religion Pages 144*

☐

Optimism *by Helen Keller*   ISBN: *1-59462-108-X*   **$15.95**

Helen Keller was blind, deaf, and mute since 19 months old, yet famously learned how to overcome these handicaps, communicate with the world, and spread her lectures promoting optimism. An inspiring read for everyone...   Biographies/Inspirational Pages 84

☐

Sara Crewe *by Frances Burnett*   ISBN: *1-59462-360-0*   **$9.45**

In the first place, Miss Minchin lived in London. Her home was a large, dull, tall one, in a large, dull square, where all the houses were alike, and all the sparrows were alike, and where all the door-knockers made the same heavy sound...   Childrens/Classic Pages 88

☐

The Autobiography of Benjamin Franklin *by Benjamin Franklin*   ISBN: *1-59462-135-7*   **$24.95**

The Autobiography of Benjamin Franklin has probably been more extensively read than any other American historical work, and no other book of its kind has had such ups and downs of fortune. Franklin lived for many years in England, where he was agent...   Biographies/History Pages 332

☐

Name	
Email	
Telephone	
Address	
City, State ZIP	

☐ **Credit Card**   ☐ **Check / Money Order**

Credit Card Number	
Expiration Date	
Signature	

Please Mail to: *Book Jungle*
PO Box 2226
Champaign, IL 61825
or Fax to: *630-214-0564*

ORDERING INFORMATION

web*: www.bookjungle.com*
email*: sales@bookjungle.com*
fax*: 630-214-0564*
mail*: Book Jungle PO Box 2226 Champaign, IL 61825*
or PayPal *to sales@bookjungle.com*

Please contact us for bulk discounts

DIRECT-ORDER TERMS

**20% Discount if You Order
Two or More Books**
Free Domestic Shipping!
Accepted: Master Card, Visa,
Discover, American Express